"GO, JORDY, GO!"

I knew there was going to be a crowd, but I wasn't prepared for the hundreds of people in the park. They were sitting in lawn chairs around the ramp or on blankets on the hills. It looked like the whole town to me. My brain was trying to convince my legs that they should run away.

I clipped on the chin strap and made my way to the ramp. As I started to climb the stairs, the cheering began. It started as a low roar and climbed through medium roar into a symphony of calls and whistles. By the time I reached the platform, every seventh-grade student in the crowd was hollering . . .

Can You Teach Me To
PICK MY NOSE?

MARTYN GODFREY

AN AVON FLARE BOOK

CAN YOU TEACH ME TO PICK MY NOSE? is an original publication of Avon Books. This work has never before appeared in book form.

AVON BOOKS
A division of
The Hearst Corporation
1350 Avenue of the Americas
New York, New York 10019

Copyright © 1990 by Martyn Godfrey
Published by arrangement with the author
Library of Congress Catalog Card Number: 89-92490
ISBN: 0-380-75915-2
RL: 5.4

First Avon Flare Printing: June 1990

AVON FLARE TRADEMARK REG. U.S. PAT. OFF. AND IN OTHER COUNTRIES, MARCA REGISTRADA, HECHO EN U.S.A.

Printed in the U.S.A.

RA   10 9 8 7 6

For my sister, Dale, B.F.B.P.

Chapter One

Welcome to Flower Valley

"I'm not sure, Chris. All of a sudden, it doesn't seem like such a good idea."

Chris frowned. "Don't tighten up on me, Jordy. Let's *parrrrrty.*" He pointed toward the house. "Listen to the music. Listen to the kids laughing. We are going to have major fun."

I looked at the Powell's place. Rock music thudded through the walls. Laughter flowed out the open door.

"But we're not invited," I said.

"I told you. That doesn't matter. They invited my brother, Reese."

"Steve Powell is in ninth grade. He doesn't want us seventh graders crashing his party."

"Stop wimping out," Chris said. "Have I ever messed you up before? Haven't I been your number-one friend since you got here?"

That was true. Chris's friendship had eased me into my new school, new town, new state, and new life.

Up until June, I'd lived in Great Falls, Montana. I'd been happy there.

Our house was in an O.K. neighborhood. It was small, but big enough for my mother, Alison, and me.

I didn't have any big hassles with Mom. Alison was a great little sister . . . lots of fun. My father

1

called me on the phone every week and visited us three or four times a year, whenever he was in town.

I did all right at school, was student council rep for my sixth grade class, and had a load of friends. I played hockey in the winter and softball in the summer.

All in all, things were pretty good for me. No problems.

But in the spring, my mother blew my life into little pieces.

"We're moving to California," she announced. "I've accepted a teaching job with the school board in a lovely town called Flower Valley. We'll make new friends. The weather will be much nicer. We'll . . ." And so on.

I was stunned. I didn't want to move. Why hadn't Mom discussed it with me? I protested loud and long, but my mother kept a cheery smile in spite of my rudeness. I tried to coax Alison on my side but she figured that moving to California was a big adventure.

"I know that you're upset, Jordy," Mom said. "You've told me that many, many times. But I'm your mother and I decide what is best for our family. I think moving to California is definitely the best thing for us."

Summer was unreal . . . packing half my stuff, throwing out the other half to save space in the U-Haul, saying good-bye to the people I'd grown up with in Great Falls, saying good-bye to Dad and wondering when I'd ever see him again, driving to Seattle, down the Pacific Coast, turning inland from San Francisco . . . unreal.

Once we'd moved into the condo and unpacked, my mother wanted me to go out and make friends. No way. I protested by staying in the house all day and watching *Gilligan's Island* and *The Flintstones* reruns.

If I'd had another month to sulk, I might have turned into a basket case. But September came and Chris saved me. He was in front of me in the registration line at John F. Kennedy Junior High on the first day of school.

We were standing in the R-Z line. Someone called Chris's name and he turned around to wave a greeting. Then he glanced at me.

"You're new," he said. "You're not from Flower Valley, are you?"

I shook my head. "I'm from Great Falls."

"Huh?"

"Great Falls, Montana," I explained.

"Right, Montana." Then he broke into a wide grin. "Well, welcome to Flower Valley. My name's Chris Williamson."

"Jordy," I told him. "Jordy Shepherd."

He shook my hand. "Allow me to be your guide to this fine educational institution."

We were in the same homeroom, and as we went through our morning classes Chris introduced me to a lot of other seventh graders. And many of the eighth and ninth graders as well.

"My brother Reese was student president here last year," he explained. "Reese has everything going for him, good looks, great athlete, good sense of humor. Just like me."

Chris started to laugh at himself. "Anyway," he went on, "when I was in sixth grade, Reese got me passes for the dances and stuff. I think I know most of the kids in the school."

We ate lunch together in the school cafeteria. "How did you know I wasn't from Flower Valley?" I asked.

"Well," he explained as he waved a half-eaten burrito in my face, "I don't want this to make you mad, but the obvious clue is that you look like a bit of a dip."

"A dip?" I said.

"Maybe that's the wrong word. What I mean is, you don't look the same as everybody else. Jeans and cowboy boots don't quite fit the Flower Valley image. I think that you'd look a lot better in some bright baggies. Some jammers. Like the guys in line."

I looked at a group of eighth graders with baggy, splash-colored, below-the-knee shorts.

"And I think that you'd look better with a different t-shirt," he went on.

"What's wrong with mine?"

He pointed at the front. "What's the Tyrell Museum of Paleontology? Why would you want to walk around with a t-shirt that says 'The Tyrell Museum of Paleontology' on it?"

I looked at my chest. "It's a terrific museum in Alberta, Canada," I said. "My dad took me there once. It's got the best dinosaur skeletons in the whole world."

"That may be," he agreed, "but it's dumb to wear a t-shirt from the place. What do you think when you see some kid wearing a t-shirt that says, 'Grandma and Grandpa visited Hawaii and all I got was this stinking shirt'?"

"I have one of those," I told him. "But I don't wear it," I added quickly. "I think it's stupid."

"Right." Chris nodded. "Think the same about the one you have on."

"What should I wear?"

"Graphics," he said. "Something you'd want painted on the bottom of a skateboard."

He pointed at his shirt. "See this. This is the symbol of Team Neeko, one of the best pro skateboard teams in the country. Now this is radical."

"Is there anything else wrong with me?" I wondered.

"I don't want to get you angry, but, yeah . . . your hair. What do you call it?"

"What do I call it?"

He nodded. "It just sits there."

"It's my hair."

"It doesn't do anything. Why don't you grow it long and bleach the back? Or maybe razor the sides like mine."

"I don't think my mom would let me do that."

He finished the burrito and swallowed. "Look, Jordy, when it comes to mothers and haircuts and clothes, you go out and do it, then you ask if it's all right."

"My mother's a teacher," I told him.

"Oh, that's too bad," he said sympathetically.

"A third grade teacher."

"Oh, I understand then," he said. "How'd she end up teaching third grade in Flower Valley? It's a long way from Montana."

"She thought it was a good move for the family . . ." I started. And then I told him about my anger and frustration about leaving my home.

Chris listened to me, nodded at some parts, shook his head at others. When I was finished, I felt better than I had in half a year, and I felt that we'd just become friends.

He came to my house after school and backed me up when I explained to my mom that my clothes and hair made me a center-shot. She smiled at me, then at Chris.

5

"I guess we're all making changes," she said as she handed me a fifty dollar bill. "Chris, would you take Jordy to the mall and help him pick out some new clothes? And maybe you can take him to the place where you get your hair cut. Perhaps Jordy would like to have his cut like yours?"

"Thanks, Mom," I said.

She made a wide grin. "My pleasure. I'm so glad to see you interested in *something* again."

So I owed to Chris the fact that I'd survived the first month of junior high, made friends, been accepted, and started liking Flower Valley.

But that didn't help me feel good about crashing Steve Powell's party.

Chapter Two

The Ninth Graders

"Come on," Chris reasoned. "I'm going to the party. If you chicken out, think of what you'll miss."

I looked at the house again.

He gave me a gentle poke in the ribs. "I know that right now you're thinking about Marissa Powell."

I blushed. "How . . ."

"I'm your friend. I can see the way you look at her in English. Your eyes drop out of your head and you get this puppy look."

I went redder.

Marissa Powell is in another seventh grade homeroom, but because of our schedules, we have the same English class with Mr. Eshenko. She's gorgeous . . . long blond hair, pale blue eyes, kind of a pouting smile, and a body that's filled out in the right places. I'd love to talk to her, but she's so popular that she's never alone. There's always a crowd of ninth grade boys around her locker.

"Hey, it's O.K., Jordy." Chris winked. "You're allowed to like girls. And you're allowed to like one girl more than the others."

"What are you guys doing?" someone interrupted. The voice belonged to Pamela Loseth, a girl in our homeroom. "Are the bozo boys looking for a little action?"

* * *

Pamela is what my mother calls a *character*. She's a head shorter than most of the girls in the class and completely different from Marissa Powell. Completely. She might have been decent-looking, but she hid her face behind awful purple-frame glasses. They didn't suit her at all. The color clashed with her hair. It was red, more apple-colored than carrot, and chopped real short on one side. The longer side was brushed over the shorter side.

If my mother was writing a report card on Pamela, she'd mention the lack of "social skills." That's teacher-talk to politely describe someone who doesn't get along with other people.

Every time Pamela spoke to someone, she was rude or weird or both.

On the second day of school, when I came to school with my new spiked hair and jammer shorts, Pamela had stopped by my locker at lunchtime.

"You look stupid," she told me.

"Pardon?"

"Your head. And the pants. What's the matter? Did Dopey die? Seven Dwarfs need a replacement?"

Then she started with a nerdy laugh, sucking a breath through her nose between each chuckle.

"Pardon me?" I figured she was joking.

"I liked you better yesterday. Your cowboy thing. It was different."

I made an embarrassed smile. "Is this real?"

"What? Kennedy Junior High? Flower Valley? The world? The universe? *Star Trek: The Next Generation?*"

"I . . . I . . . What are you talking about?"

"Gotta go," she'd grinned. "Take some advice. Grow the hair back." Then she'd charged off down the hall.

From what I'd overheard, her conversations with other kids were similar. Not many people seemed to like her.

"So what are the bozo boys up to?" Pamela repeated.

"Go away," Chris said. "You're attracting flies."

She laughed. Ha-hork. Ha-hork.

"Bug off!" Chris insisted.

"You know, you'd be even funnier with a lobotomy," she chuckled.

"Let's go." Chris grabbed my shirt.

"You going to Steve's party to check out Marissa, right?" Pamela asked. "Ms. Bubblehead of Flower Valley. Maybe hope for a little kissy-face?"

"Go play in traffic," Chris called as he pushed me toward the Powell's door.

"You should be able to think up something better than that, Chris," she called back.

So Chris said something disgusting.

"Show me how and I'll try it," she hollered back. Then she *ha-horked* a last time and half-jogged down the street.

"Fruit salad," Chris said. "Got to watch out for that one, Jordy. Future tenant of the Bates Motel."

"The what?"

"The Bates Motel. You know, *Psycho*. The guy who dresses up like his mother . . . forget it. Why are we talking movies when we have Marissa Powell just a few feet away? Let's go."

And so, still full of doubt, I reluctantly followed him to the front door.

Chris knocked on the open door and poked his head into the hallway. "Let me do the talking," he said. "I've got a way with words."

Mr. Powell suddenly filled the doorway. "Chris!"

he boomed. "I hardly recognized you. You've grown a foot since last year."

"Still only got two." Chris smiled.

Mr. Powell laughed. "That's a good one. You have a sense of humor just like your brother. How is Reese? I hear that he's all set for the football team."

"He's on for sure," Chris said. "Number One."

"That'll make him the first freshman quarterback at Flower Valley High." Mr. Powell was bragging as if he was Reese's father. "What a brother you've got."

"He's something else," Chris agreed.

Mr. Powell looked at me. "And who's this?"

"Jordy Shepherd." I introduced myself. "I'm a friend of Chris's."

"And a real big friend of Reese," Chris said. "Reese says that Jordy here is a natural football player. Every night Reese gives Jordy tips."

"Really?" Mr. Powell seemed impressed. He shook my hand. "What can I do for you boys?"

"Well," Chris said, smiling. "We heard that Steve was having a party. He invited Reese. And since Reese can't come, we wondered if it would be all right to take his place?"

Mr. Powell made a wry smile. "Why not." Then he pointed down the hallway. "The party is in the family room and out back. Have fun."

"Football?" I whispered to Chris as we walked down the hall. "I don't play football. And I've only met Reese a couple of times. We've never talked about football."

"I know," Chris whispered back. "Mr. Powell is a football freak. I was helping to make an impression for you. Like I said, I got a way with words."

"But, I don't think . . ."

"It's party time!" Chris shouted as we entered the family room.

The room was jammed with kids. They were sitting on the couch, leaning against the wall, and bunched around the CD. Everyone was sipping sodas or talking. Outside on the patio, the speakers pounded Mötley Crüe for a dozen dancers.

As soon as we entered, I felt like I wanted to fade away. *En masse,* the kids turned to examine us. I knew the faces, even though I didn't know all the names. They were *the* ninth graders. The people who sat at the cafeteria table near the window. The ones who ran the student council and social committee. The guys and girls on the sports teams. The ones with the right clothes. *The* group.

The noise level dropped as they noticed us. Ugly looks crossed some faces. The rest looked stunned.

"Hey, everyone," Chris waved.

"What are you doing here?!" Steve Powell shouted from the crowd by the CD player. He wasn't pleased to see us. In fact, he looked extremely angry.

Chapter Three

A Skateboard Champion?

Steve folded his arms over his chest and glared at us. "Who invited you?" he snarled.

Chris didn't answer the question. Instead he asked one of his own. "How's the old skateboard?" Then he turned to me. "You know what, Jordy? Steve is one of the best thrashers in the school. A king of skateboards."

Other kids shuffled behind Steve. Heavy metal thudded against the windows.

"Yeah," Chris announced to everyone. "Steve Powell is one of the best."

"Cut the crap. What are you doing here?" Steve repeated.

Chris looked puzzled. "You invited Reese, didn't you?"

"So what?" Steve scowled. "What's that got to do with you?"

"Reese can't make it," Chris explained. "He told Jordy and me to come instead."

"Reese *told* you to come?" Steve asked.

Chris nodded. " 'Go say hello for me' is what my brother said."

Steve squinted and then nodded once. "O.K., but you better not be feeding me. Next time I see Reese I'm going to ask him. If you're feeding me . . ." He let the threat fade into a nasty sneer.

Steve returned to the CD and slowly the room returned to a party buzz.

Chris made his way to the cooler and removed two Cokes. He handed one to me. "See"—he smiled—"I told you it would be no problem."

"No problem? What's all this stuff about your brother *telling* us to go. He didn't say that, did he?"

"Not so loud," Chris warned. "Don't worry about it. Reese will cover me."

He popped the tab on the can and went out to the patio. I chucked my Coke back into the ice and turned to leave. Maybe Chris could feel that he belonged at this party, but I couldn't.

Then I noticed Marissa Powell talking with a boy on the couch. She didn't seem too interested in what he was saying. She glanced at the CD group, the guys goofing around by the book shelf, the dancers outside the patio doors, a couple on the love seat who were obviously "in love," and then at me.

As soon as I saw those liquid, blue eyes staring at me, I smiled. A big, toothy, stupid grin.

Marissa didn't smile back, but she did walk over to me.

"You're in my English class, aren't you?" she asked. "I'm Marissa."

"I know," I said. "My name is Jordy."

She looked over my shoulder and checked out the dancers. "You want to dance?"

Marissa Powell just asked me to dance, I thought.

"Sure," I said. "You bet. Let's dance."

We shuffled through the patio doors. I couldn't talk to her above the thud of the guitars and drums. I don't think she would have listened to me anyway. She got into the music, shaking her head, lip-syncing the lyrics. In fact, she didn't even look at me. She might as well have been dancing by herself.

But I did enjoy watching her. The way that her long hair curled over her shoulders, the way she moved, the tiny dimples around her mouth, how well her t-shirt fit . . . everything about her.

Halfway through the third song, the music stopped. "Food!" someone yelled. I saw Mr. Powell in the family room with a tray full of tacos. The dancers shuffled into the house.

"You hungry?" Marissa asked.

"Are you?"

"No. My dad's tacos are the pits. Let's go sit down."

We moved to a picnic table next to a brick barbecue at the end of the yard. She slid onto the bench and I sat down beside her.

"How come you and Chris showed up to the party?" she asked. "How come Steve let you stay?"

I repeated Chris's lie about his brother.

"That explains it." Marissa nodded. "Steve doesn't like seventh graders. He thinks they rate below sludge worms."

"They?" I wondered. "You're in seventh grade."

"Well, not me," she explained. "I'm not like the rest of you guys, am I?"

Certainly not to me, I thought.

"Are you going with the boy you were sitting with on the couch?" I asked.

"Larry?" she said. "No. He likes me, but I can do better."

I didn't know what to say to that comment. "Do you like Mr. Eshenko?" I asked. "I think English class is really interesting, don't you?" I sounded like a little kid!

Marissa didn't get to answer. "I see you've met my new buddy, Marissa," Chris interrupted. "Jordy is a great guy."

Chris made a wink that only I could see. "Say, Marissa, did Jordy tell you what a whiz he is on a skateboard? An ultimate thrasher."

"Pardon?" I said. "I've never . . ."

"Now don't go all modest on us," Chris scolded. "You should be proud of the fact that you won the Great Falls Junior Ramp Championship."

"I what?" I muttered.

"That's terrific!" Marissa grabbed my arm and squeezed it. She was definitely excited by the news. "You know, I really admire boys who can do all those tricks on a skateboard."

"I know you do," Chris said as he gave me another secret wink.

"Oh, yes," Marissa grinned. "I think it's so exciting. Skaters really impress me."

"They do?" I said.

She nodded. "I'd like to see you on your board."

"Well, I . . ."

"Did I hear right?" Steve moved beside Chris and squinted at me. "Junior Champion of Great Falls?"

"Ramp Champion," Chris pointed out.

"You look like a poser to me," Steve snarled.

"A poser?" I said.

"No way that Jordy just stands around showing off his fancy board," Chris said quickly. "This here boy is grade A."

Steve pinched his bottom lip and regarded me. "I think you're just mouthing off to impress Marissa."

"Jordy wouldn't do that, would you?" Marissa asked as she squeezed my arm again.

What was I supposed to say now?

16

Chapter Four

We Have a Problem

I didn't have to answer. Chris did it for me. "Jordy's no poser. He's a dude."

"He doesn't look like a skater to me," Steve said.

"They look different in Montana," Chris pointed out.

"Get real, hosehead," Steve snarled. "I'll go get my board and he can prove me wrong. He can show me what a hot shot he is."

This was silly. "Now just a . . ."

"*Ramp* champion." Chris stopped me. "Jordy is *ramp* champion. He doesn't do freestyle or street. And I don't see any ramps in your backyard."

"OK," Steve said. "Then I got a idea. Hey, Larry," he called. "Come here."

The guy who'd been sharing the couch with Marissa joined us. He was munching on a taco. "What's up, Steve?" he asked.

"I want you to witness this," Steve said. Then he turned to me. "Next Saturday is the Flower Valley Skateboard Competition. Now I'm sure that it's nowhere as big as the one you won in Great Falls, but we got some good talent. And since you're a thrasher and Marissa is really impressed with that fact, I'm sure you're going to enter the contest. So, I'll bet you that I end higher in the points on the half-pipe ramp than you do."

"This is—" I began.

"You're on!" Chris agreed. "How much?"

"Now hold on . . ."

"This is exciting," Marissa said.

"How about a hundred big ones?" Steve suggested.

"A hundred dollars?" I gasped.

"How about two hundred?" Chris said.

I tried to say something but my mouth was stuck in open.

"You got the money?" Steve wondered.

"From my paper route," Chris said. "You got it?"

"I deliver for Shopper's Drugs, don't I?" Steve grumbled. "Course I got it. You're on, slimeface."

They shook hands.

I stared at Chris. He returned a confident smile.

"Can I talk to you a moment?" I said. I turned to Marissa as I stood up. "Excuse me."

I pushed Chris toward the fence. "What was all that about?"

"I'm just trying to help you impress Marissa," he explained.

"Not that! The bet with Steve."

Chris looked down and kicked at the grass. "Sometimes the guy really bothers me. Even Reese says that he needs to be cut down a peg."

Then he looked at me and winked. "Don't worry about it. Steve is good, but he's not great. Even I'm better. An average skater can beat him." He stared at me. "You are average, aren't you? I mean, they do skateboard in Montana, right?"

"Chris, I've never been on a skateboard in my life."

"Never?"

I shook my head. "When I was in fourth grade, I

asked my mom for a skateboard for my birthday. She said no. She told me that she'd seen so many kids hurt themselves on skateboards that she'd never let me have one."

"You never used your friends' boards? You never tried a ramp?"

"No. Skateboarding wasn't all that big at my school. And the principal wouldn't let the kids bring them to school anyway."

"Oh," he groaned.

I signed and glanced at Marissa. She was smiling at me. She waved, a cute little flip of her hand.

"We have a problem," Chris said.

"Not *we*. You're the one who started lying. You're the one who got into the bet. I didn't say anything."

He bit his bottom lip. "I didn't think this would happen. I know that Marissa really has a thing for guys who are hot on the boards. I was just trying to help you make the big impression. Just like when I told Mr. Powell you were a great football player. When Steve started giving us a hard time I just let things get away." He thumped the side of his head. "I didn't expect this to happen."

"And now you're going to lose two hundred dollars."

"No, I'm not," he said.

"Yes, you are," I insisted. "There is no way I'm going to be able to enter that contest. No matter how bad Steve is, he's going to be much better than me."

He looked at my sheepishly. "That doesn't have anything to do with it. I don't have two hundred dollars to lose."

"You don't have the money? What was all that talk about a paper route?"

"I spend it as soon as I get it," he confessed.

I looked into the sky and shook my head. "I don't believe this."

"We have a problem," he said again. "And it's definitely *we*. What do you think Steve will do when he finds out that I can't pay up?"

"Be reasonable about it?"

"No way. I know him. He'll pound my face into Silly Putty."

"Not if you tell him you were just joking around."

"But not just *my* face," Chris went on. "He's going to come after you as well."

"Why would he do that? I haven't done anything."

"He's going to think that you were lying about your skateboard skills so that you could hit on his sister."

"That's stupid," I said. "This whole thing is dumb. I'm going to straighten this out. Tell Steve the truth and call off the bet."

Chris grabbed my arm. "You can't do that now. You can't call off a bet once you've made it."

"When I explain . . ."

"When you explain, it'll make you look like a complete foul pole. What do you think everyone will think when they hear you were just posing, just shooting off your mouth to make an impression? Your name will be doodle at Kennedy. No one will talk to you for the next three years. Your rep will be shot."

"Me? I wasn't bragging. You were. I didn't say anything. You were the one wagging your big mouth."

"A minor detail. If you confess now, your rep is fried. I know how these things work."

"But—"

Chris didn't let me protest further. "And what will that special person think? What about Marissa?" he went on.

"This is so stupid."

"You've made the big first move with her," Chris continued. "Think of what it would be like to go to the next dance with Ms. Teeny-Wonderful of northern California."

"But—"

"Think of what she's going to think if she finds out that you're just posing?"

"Stop saying that! I didn't say anything about skateboards. I didn't pose. You posed for me."

"Marissa won't remember it that way."

"But . . . but . . . why did you go and open your dumb mouth in the first place?"

"I don't know." He shrugged. "These bluffs have always worked in the past. I didn't expect the impossible to happen. I didn't think I'd run into the one in a million chance . . . a guy who's never been on a skateboard."

"Get serious, Chris."

"O.K., let's think this out. What are we going to do?" he said.

Marissa Powell squeezed between us. "I'm getting bored. What are you talking about anyway?"

"Tactics," Chris said. "We're just trying to figure out what moves to do next Saturday to impress the judges."

Marissa put a choke hold on my arm. "Oh," she said. "I find this really exciting. Imagine . . . the Junior Champion of Great Falls, North Dakota."

"Montana," I corrected.

"Whatever," Marissa said as she tightened the grip on my arm. "Oh, I'm so anxious to see you on your board."

What was happening here? What had Chris got me into?

Chapter Five

Alison's Problem

Marissa and I danced for the rest of the evening. She tried to get me to talk about my *incredible skill*, but I shrugged it off. "It's nothing," I said, which was definitely the truth.

I didn't get a chance to talk to Chris on the weekend, to find a way to get out of the bet, because Mom took Alison and me camping in the mountains. Even though the redwoods and fir trees were beautiful and the campground overlooked a terrific lake, the skateboard problem stayed on my mind.

I thought that maybe I could go over to Steve's place and talk to him one-on-one, explain that Chris was just being a stupid seventh grader and that it had all been a misunderstanding and wasn't it funny when you think about it, ha-ha. But, as Chris pointed out, that wouldn't work. Steve would just get angry. And what would Marissa think of me? I certainly wouldn't be one of her favorite people.

I was sitting on some rocks by the lake, deep in thought, when Alison joined me to talk about her problem. "You O.K., Jordy?" she asked after she'd sat beside me. "You been real quiet."

I reached over and tousled her hair. I think Alison is such a neat-looking kid, lots of freckles, upturned nose and missing teeth. I was six years old when she was born and I loved her the moment I saw her skinny face in the hospital nursery.

"I'm great," I told her. "I'm just thinking about big kid things."

"Oh."

"Tell me what's new with you," I said. "How are things going in first grade?"

"O.K.," she told me. "Ms. Dudley is funny."

"Good." I nodded. "It's always better to have a funny teacher."

"Jordy, I got a problem with a boy. Can you help me?"

"A boy?" I smiled.

"He's stupid," she said.

"Right. One of those."

"He bugs me all the time," she said. "And I want him to stop being so stupid. I thought that since you're a boy, you can help me."

"I'll try. What does he do?"

"Stuff," she said. "Like, yesterday when we were painting, he flicked a booger at me."

"He what?"

"We were at the paint table and he picked his nose. Then he rolled it in a ball and flicked it at me. It bounced off. Right here." She pointed at her chin.

"The dirty little brat," I said. "That's disgusting."

"He did it twice. The second one hit me here." She pointed above her left eye. "What should I do?"

"Well, you could tell Ms. Dudley," I advised. "But . . . you know what? When I was in first grade, there was this girl called Carol-Ann James. I really liked Carol-Ann and I wanted to be her friend. But I didn't know how to go about getting her attention. So you know what I did?"

"What?" Alison said.

24

"I punched her arm. Everytime I saw her, I punched on her arm. You see, I wanted her to notice me."

"Did you make friends with her?"

I shook my head. "After two days of pounding her arms, Carol-Ann hated my guts. And I got sent to the principal's office. A real mess."

"What's that got to do with Roger?" Alison wondered.

"Well, maybe flicking boogers at you is Roger's way of telling you that he wants to be your friend."

"That's stupid."

"He's a stupid boy, right? Maybe you can get him to stop, if you tell him you'd like to be his friend. You don't hate him, do you?"

"I just want him to stop acting so dumb," she told me.

"Go for it then," I suggested. "Just say, 'Roger, would you like to be my friend?' "

"You think that'll make him stop?"

"It's worth a try," I said.

"O.K., thanks, Jordy."

"I'm curious. What else had he done to bug you?"

"Well, we had games in the gym and Ms. Dudley made Roger captain of one of the teams and he didn't pick me."

I hid my smile. "I can see how that would upset you."

"On Friday, he took my sandwich out of my lunchbox and sat on it."

"Then again, perhaps you should just bop this guy on the head with something heavy. Get him to smarten up."

"What?"

"Nothing. It sure sounds like Roger wants a friend," I said.

She nodded. "Jordy, what's big kid things?"

"This and that," I told her. "For one thing, there's a girl at school that I'd really like to be my friend. I'd like her to be my girlfriend. You know, my *girlfriend* girlfriend."

"To take out on dates?"

"Not real dates, but more-or-less like that."

"Yuck!"

"Wait six years and you'll think different."

"What's her name?" Alison asked.

"Marissa."

"That's a nice name. What's she like? Is she in your class?"

"She's in one of my classes. And she's really pretty, super-cute."

"What else?"

"Well, she likes to watch people skateboard."

"And?"

"And that's all I know about her right now."

"You going to kiss her and stuff?"

"That's my business."

"Yuck!"

"Tell me more about Roger. Is he a good-looking guy?"

She shook her head. "No way! He's ugly! But he's always laughing. He's real happy all the time."

"I suppose a kid who's into flicking boogers will find all sorts of things funny. Say, you want to go for a walk with me?"

"Yeah, I'd like that."

Alison's problem sidetracked me for a while. When we got back late on Sunday night, the skateboard thing had lost some of its urgency. I fell asleep thinking that I was going to go to school on Monday and somehow be able to get a grip on everything.

I didn't know how wrong I could be.

Chapter Six

The Seventh Grade Champion

I was walking into school on Monday morning when an overweight kid from Marissa's homeroom blocked my way.

"Hey, my main man." He grinned as he gave me a high five. "My name is Clarence Boyer. I want to wish you good luck on Saturday. I heard about the skateboard bet with that ninth grader, Steve Powell."

"You heard? When did you hear?"

"Oh, sometime on the weekend. Look, I just want to say that I'm with you."

"Well, er . . . thanks."

"Right," he went on. "With you all the way. I want to see you beat that guy real bad. He and his buddies have been giving me a hard time. You know, about my weight. I'm glad you're going to grind his gears."

I tried to talk to Chris in homeroom, but I was virtually mobbed by classmates who wanted to offer their support.

It soon became obvious that *most* of the kids knew about the bet. And in English class, Mr. Eshenko made sure *everyone* knew.

"Well, here he is," he announced to the class. "Jordy Shepherd, the seventh grade champion."

A few of the guys cheered. I looked over at Chris. He was chewing his pen and staring at the floor.

"I heard about the bet," Mr. Eshenko went on. "So you're going to defend the honor of the seventh graders? Glad to hear it. It's good to see someone take on the ninth graders. The seventh grade homeroom teachers will all be cheering for you."

I cringed and glanced at Chris again. He was still studying the floor tiles.

"In fact, from the talk in the staff room, most of us plan to be at the skateboard competition to watch this," Mr. Eshenko told me. "The contest is always fun. You and Steve going face-to-face will make it all the more interesting."

Then he turned his attention to Marissa. "And how are you going to cheer?" he asked her. "For your brother or your classmate?"

"Well," she said, smiling, "I suppose I should be loyal to my family. But considering the honor of my grade is at stake, I hope Jordy wins." Then she paused and winked at me. "Besides, Jordy is cuter than Steve."

Several girls and guys hooted at that.

Mr. Eshenko laughed. "This kind of stuff is good for school spirit," he said. "Great Falls' loss is Flower Valley's gain."

Again some cheers. And again Chris wouldn't look at me.

At lunch, I threw my books into my locker and slammed the door. The hall monitor gave me a nasty look. So what? I didn't care if I got a detention. Where was Chris?

I was about to stomp into the cafeteria, but Pamela Loseth blocked my way. "Hey, Jordy," she said.

"Get out of my way," I growled. "I've got to go see somebody."

She ignored me. "You want some advice?"

"No." I shoved past her.

"Dopey haircut means goofy brains, huh?" she called after me.

I pushed my way into the cafeteria and saw Chris sitting at a corner table. He was backed against the wall as if he was trying to hide from somebody. I knew who the somebody was.

When he saw me charging at him, he made a weak smile and waved half a sandwich.

"Hi, Jordy," he said. "I've been wanting to talk to you all morning."

"Bull feathers!"

"Oh, I have. But you've been so busy. You've turned into quite the celebrity."

"So let's talk now. Outside!"

He pointed at the table. "I'm eating my lunch."

I grabbed what was left of his sandwich, the Twinkies, and the chocolate milk and dumped it all in the garbage. "Not anymore."

"O.K." He stood up. "I can tell you're upset, but that was my lunch."

"I'm more important. Let's go."

We went behind the school and Chris sat on the steps near the service doors. I paced in front of him.

"We should have called off the bet on Friday." I was almost shouting. "I didn't think it would get this out of hand. All the kids in the school know about it. And the teachers are going to cheer for me."

"It's amazing how word gets around," he agreed.

"Come Saturday, I'm going to look like the biggest jerk in the whole country. We have to call off the bet."

"We've been through that," Chris pointed out. "Think of your rep. Think of Marissa."

"Think of what will happen to my rep on Saturday.

Think of Marissa's reaction when she sees me try to get on a skateboard and then fall flat on my butt. We have to confess now. Tell everyone it was your big mouth that got out of hand.''

"I told you. No one will understand," Chris insisted. "Besides while you were away this weekend, I thought of a way to get us out of this with honor. Sit down and let me explain it."

I sighed and plonked beside him. "All right. Go ahead."

"Well," Chris began, "I figure this can't fail . . ."

Chapter Seven

Wet and Slimy

As soon as Mom left for work the next morning, I phoned Chris. "I'm alone," I told him. "You can come over now."

Ten minutes later Chris was unloading the contents of a plastic shopping bag onto the kitchen counter. "Where's your little sister?" he asked. "Do you have to take her to school?"

"Alison goes to the same school where my mom—works. The poor kid gets to go early and stay late. Wait until I tell you about this kid in her class."

"Tell me later," he said. "And take your sock off. I can't do it over a sock, can I?"

"I'm still not sure that this will work," I said as I pulled off my left sock. "Steve is going to be suspicious."

"So what?" Chris reasoned. "How is he going to prove it's fake? It's the best plan. It'll get us out of the bet and save your rep."

He ran some water into the sink. Then he ripped open one if the boxes that had been in the plastic bag and began to unroll a bandage. "This is really easy. Reese showed me how to do it last night. The bandage is covered with plaster of Paris. We just cut off a piece, soak it, and wrap it around your ankle. When it dries, we have a cast. And you can't skateboard wearing a cast, can you?"

"I can't skateboard without one either," I said. "How did Reese get the stuff?"

"He bought it at the drug store. I have to pay him back when I get my paper route money. You ready?"

I watched Chris wet the bandage and then place it carefully around my left ankle. It felt cold and slimy. Drops of milky water fell on the kitchen floor. He grabbed a paper towel and placed it under my ankle. "This won't take long. I can remember how the doctor did it when I broke my wrist in fourth grade. I fell off my skateboard."

"I've never seen you use your skateboard," I told him. "You good at it?"

He shook his head. "Not really. I try, but I'm no better than average. I can't even acid drop properly."

"Acid drop?"

"It's a trick. A basic move. You don't know what it means, huh?"

"No."

"Then it's a good job you broke your ankle, isn't it?" He winked.

"If everyone believes it."

"You ever broken anything for real?"

I shook my head and watched him repeat the procedure with a second piece of plaster bandage.

"It hurts," he said. "But it's a good thing in a way. I don't mean the busted bone. I mean the sympathy you get from your folks. I was treated great for the six weeks I had to keep the cast on."

"Six weeks! You didn't say anything about six weeks. I can't keep this thing on for that long. You said only a day."

"I was wrong about that part. I read up on it last night. We can't take it off until Friday. Then you can wear a pressure bandage. That's what it says about hairline fractures in the medical book I checked in the library. We've still got all the bases covered."

"What am I going to tell my mother?" I asked. "How am I going to wear it around the house for the next four days?"

"No sweat. Mr. Eshenko is going to assign those comedy skits today, right? You can tell her you're wearing it for the skit in English class."

"She won't believe it. Not my mom."

"Sure she will," he assured me. "Just remember to tell her that you're practicing every day and the most practical thing is to keep it on. Then tell her that you're getting lots of attention from the girls in the other classes who think you've really broken your ankle. She'll understand that."

"I want all this to go away."

"By lunchtime, it'll be a memory," he said as he twisted a third strip around my ankle.

Chris changed the subject. "You ever find it hard with your mom and little sister?"

"What do you mean?"

"Well, you got nobody to talk to. If something's bugging me, I can go and speak to Reese or my dad. You don't have a dad to talk to."

"I talk to my mom about important stuff," I told him.

"But it's not like talking to your old man, is it?"

"To tell the truth, I'm not sure. I don't think I've ever talked to my dad about anything serious. He's not the type."

Chris placed a piece of rubber against my heel and wrapped another piece of tape around the edge to hold it in place. "This is a tire from one of my old Tonka trucks. It'll make it look like a walking cast."

"I'm putting my trust in your skill, doctor."

35

He chuckled. "Tell me more about your family. When did your folks split up?"

"Just before Alison was born."

"You remember what it was like?"

"Hardly anything. I can't remember them fighting. I can't remember any fireworks. And the funny thing is, I can't really remember any good times either. It's like my father never lived with us."

"You were kind of young," he pointed out. "You ever visit him? He ever see you and Alison?"

"Three, maybe four times a year. Whenever he was in Great Falls, he'd drop by to say hello. He and Mom get along really well."

"No kidding. My mom was married to some guy for a couple of years before my dad. She never sees him. Says that she hopes she never runs into him again."

"I think my parents still love each other," I told him. "I can tell by the way they joke around."

"That doesn't make sense. Why get a divorce if you're in love?"

"I think it's because loving somebody is one thing, but living with him is another. Do you know what I mean?"

"I guess."

"My mom and dad are so different. She's a teacher, usually strict and extremely organized. My father is a ranch hand and drifts between jobs in Montana and Canada."

"Hey, that's neat. Your old man is a cowboy."

"What passes for a cowboy nowadays," I agreed. "You see, I think when he and Mom first met, he loved her so much that he tried to settle down in the city, get a regular job, start a family."

"And he missed the cows?" Chris said as he added

a large piece of wet plaster to the now substantial cast.

"I think he felt tied down. Being in love wasn't enough for him."

"That's interesting. You ever think of falling in love, Jordy?"

"No. But I think about having a girlfriend."

"Marissa Powell." He smiled.

"Right. Marissa for me and maybe Pamela Loseth for you. We could double-date."

Chris made like he was throwing up and we both started to laugh.

"She's not that bad," I chuckled.

He pretended to throw up again and that made me laugh even more.

It was a good minute before we settled down. As I was catching my breath, I studied the cast. "Don't put any more tape on, Chris. It's getting heavy."

"Maybe I should save the tape for Pamela's face," he suggested.

"That's not funny," I said with a smile. "Now you're getting nasty."

"Well, excuse me!" he said in a Steve Martin imitation. "Where's your hair dryer? That'll speed things up."

A half hour later, I was looking at an awful semidry monstrosity that was welded to my foot.

Chapter Eight

It's All Bulgy

"That looks terrible," I groaned.

Chris didn't say anything for several moments. "Oh, I don't know. It's not that bad."

"Get serious. It's all bulgy on one side."

"Bulgy?" he said. "What kind of word is *bulgy?"*

"It's not even. It's lopsided. The pieces of tape go every which way. It's jagged on the edges. There's great glops of plaster all over it."

He looked hurt. "Are you saying you don't like it?"

"I'm saying that it looks stupid! Who is going to believe that a doctor did that?"

"We'll tell everybody that it was an intern," he said. "We'll say it was his first day on the job and he'd been up for seventy-two hours."

"Right," I snarled. "It just doesn't look real. I've seen guys in walking casts before. They didn't look anything like that."

"You're being too critical, Jordy. Honest, it doesn't look that bad. Tell you what, why don't I get a Magic Marker and write a bunch of fake signatures all over it."

"And who would have signed it since last night? Who are the 'bunch'?"

"Let's start walking to school then. We'll try it out on a few kids. I'm sure they'll believe it."

"No way. You have to do it again."

"There's no time," he said. Then he held up his right hand and crossed his heart with his left. "Honest. It doesn't look that bad. Steve Powell will buy it."

"I don't think—"

"I got it. I'll run home and get one of my Dad's grey wool socks. He wears them inside his waders when he goes fishing. They're huge. We'll stretch it over the cast and cut a little hole for the Tonka tire. I'll buy him some new socks when I get my paper money. What do you think of that?"

A short time later, I was hobbling down the street with his father's grey sock stretched over the cast. I had to admit that it looked real now. The sock covered the disaster. Maybe we *could* convince Steve Powell that I was unable to compete against him on Saturday.

"You got the story straight?" Chris asked as we turned the corner.

"Sure," I answered. "I was practicing on the ramp in the park and broke my ankle."

"Hairline fracture," he corrected. "That way we can take the cast off on Friday."

"I don't even know what the ramp looks like," I said.

Someone was humming behind us. I shuffled to one side to let the person pass. Instead I heard a familiar voice.

"Hey, it's the bozo brothers."

"And it's Miss Congeniality," Chris replied.

Pamela made one ha-hork and took a close look at my sock-cast. Then she stared into my face. Then back at my cast. Then into my face. "How'd you do that?" she asked.

"It's a hairline fracture," I told her. "I did it last night on the ramp in the park. I sort of went head-over-heels. When I tried to stand up, there was this terrible pain."

Chris gave me a thumbs up sign to tell me that I'd done a good job.

Pamela squinted into my face. "Steve won't believe you," she said matter-of-factly.

"So what?" Chris said. "It's the truth. If he doesn't believe the truth, then it's his problem."

"Steve will *know* that you're sucking out." She grinned.

"What are you talking about?" I asked.

"Well, how do you know that it's broken?"

"We went to the hospital and had an X ray," I lied. "Then the doctor put on the cast."

"So Mrs. Powell knows you were there then?" She moved her face closer to my face.

"What do you mean by that?" I backed up.

"I mean that my mother was the doctor on the night shift in Emergency last night. This morning when she came home, she said that it had been a quiet night. In fact, she said that she and the emergency nurse had managed to get caught up on all their paperwork. Guess who the nurse was?"

"Steve's mom?" I asked.

She nodded. "See, Steve won't believe you."

I swore and began to clump back to my house.

"Don't worry, Dopey," Pamela called after me. "I won't tell anybody what you tried to do."

I unlocked the door, charged into the kitchen, grabbed the scissors, and began to hack at the cast. "I knew it was a stupid idea. I *knew* it. What I was thinking about. My mom never would have believed me anyway. Wearing it for a comedy skit? Why did I ever think it would work?"

"Take it easy with those things," Chris said. "Don't cut yourself."

I continued to bash at the hard plaster. "What am I going to do now? How am I going to face everyone?"

"Pamela won't tell anybody. You heard her."

"It's not Pamela I'm worried about. It's this Saturday!"

A large piece of cast fell onto the floor.

"Maybe you'd better let me do that," Chris suggested. "Or the next piece that falls off is going to be part of your body."

I looked at the scissors and the chewed-up cast. I hadn't realized I was so upset. I handed them to Chris.

"What a stupid thing to try," I repeated.

Chris began to gently chip at the plaster. "It was a good idea. What was the chance of Steve Powell's mom being on shift in Emergency? It was a weird coincidence." He peeled half the cast away. "We haven't lost the war yet. This is just a minor setback. We'll go to school, think about it, and by tonight we'll have another idea. We'll find a way to save your rep and my money."

Chapter Nine

Mr. Slick Wheels

We were late for school. As the assistant principal was writing my late slip, she said, "Oh, yes, Jordy Shepherd. You're the skateboard champion from up north. I'm looking forward to seeing you on Saturday. I suppose you're late because you were practicing."

I needed that.

And when I got to English class, I found all the kids wearing tags which read, "Go, Jordy, Go! Seventh Graders Rule!" Even Mr. Eshenko sported one. I soon discovered that Marissa had made them up.

I needed that as well.

I met Marissa by her locker at lunchtime. "You O.K., Jordy?" she asked as we moved through the cafeteria line. "You haven't said that you like the tags I made last night. It was almost midnight by the time I finished."

"They're real nice," I mumbled.

"I thought of what to write on them all by myself."

"Very creative. And original."

She grinned at me, full of pride.

Pamela Loseth elbowed me in the ribs and I almost dropped my tray. She waved a carton of chocolate milk in the air. "I'm going to tell the cashier that you're going to pay for this. I figure you owe it to me since I saved you this morning. Thanks." She saluted and moved to the cashier.

"What was that all about?" Marissa wondered.

"I owe her some money," I lied. "She was just reminding me about it in her usual way."

"She's such a loser, isn't she?" Marissa scrunched her nose as if she'd just smelled the biggest fart in the whole world. "I mean I just couldn't stand it if I was *her*. Can you imagine having to spend your entire life as Pamela Loseth?"

We paid for our lunches and sat at a table of kids from Marissa's homeroom.

I watched Marissa eat. It was neat the way she took small bites. You could hardly make out that she was chewing. This struck me as cute. In fact, there wasn't much about Marissa that didn't strike me as cute.

At one point in the meal, she leaned forward and began to whisper. "All of the kids are looking at us. Everyone is so jealous of us."

I glanced at the other tables. There were a lot of people watching us.

"Isn't it exciting?" She giggled.

"Yes," I said. *No,* I thought.

"All the girls wish they were me. I mean, I'm going out with *the* ramp skateboard champion. And all the boys wish they were you. You're going with the best-looking girl in the school."

"We're going together?" I asked.

"Well, not really," she said. "But since you're the most important boy in seventh grade this week, then it's only natural that you and I should be together, isn't it?"

"I suppose so."

"And on Saturday, if you win, then we can make it official."

"If I win, then we're going together?"

"That would only be right, wouldn't it?"

44

"Hey, poser!" Steve Powell stood beside me. He had a brightly colored skateboard with phosphorescent green wheels tucked under his left arm.

"Hello, Steve." Marissa smiled at her brother.

Steve acknowledged her greeting with a grunt. Then he leaned his right hand on the table and bent his head to the side the way a dog does when it's listening to something. Everyone at the table . . . in fact, everyone in the cafeteria . . . was watching him.

"You know what?" he said. "I have yet to see you on your board. In fact, I have yet to see your board. I don't even think you got a board. I think your just strutting around pretending that you're Mister Slick Wheels to impress the girls."

Chris got up from his table and jogged toward us. "What's the matter, Steve?" he attacked. "You starting to feel scared? You think that you can intimidate Jordy here by talking tough? He may be in seventh grade, but he isn't going to be pysched-out just because a ninth grade clown is dumping on him."

There was a loud and boisterous cheer from the seventh grade tables.

"Way to tell him," someone shouted.

Steve gave that kid the finger.

"I'm just calling what I see," he went on. "I see a poser sitting with my sister. I'm putting up with that because, come Saturday, I'm going to win two hundred bucks from your jerkface friend. And when everyone watches you and finds out you're posing, then I might just make Jello out of your brains."

"Tough talk!" Chris said. "And it'll just make you look like more of a dipstick after you lose."

Steve turned his attention to my friend. "You're pushing it. Just 'cause you're Reese's brother doesn't

45

make you Superboy. Maybe I'll put your face on up-side down as well."

"The monitor just came in," somebody called.

"Saturday!" Steve snarled. Then he twisted around and marched out of the cafeteria.

"Steve can be really mean when he's mad," Marissa said.

I rubbed my temples and sighed. "That really cheers me."

Chapter Ten

Another Jordy Shepherd?

That afternoon, we had English class and Pamela Loseth got put in *her* place.

We'd been studying comedy sketches all week, listening to Abbott and Costello do their "Who's On First?" routine, studying old Marx brothers films, watching the MacKenzie brothers on SCTV reruns, stuff like that. And we'd been trying to write our own funny stories.

"Well," Mr. Eshenko told us, "we've been entertained long enough. Now, as I told you, it's time for us to start our major assignment on this unit. I want you to find a partner to work with. Pick somebody you get along with because you'll both receive the same mark. Next Monday, I want you to hand in a script for a comedy sketch for two people."

A few of the kids groaned, including me.

"And," he went on, "I'm going to want you and your partner to perform the sketch as well."

More groans.

"All right, find yourself a partner."

My mom told me that she never does this. She always assigns people as partners. She says there's always one person in every class who no one wants in his group or on his team.

Chris and I paired off, although I thought Marissa and I would have made a terrific duet. She chose her friend, Jennifer, as her partner. All the other kids doubled up just as quickly. All except Pamela Loseth. She was the person no one wanted.

Mr. Eshenko said that he wouldn't mind a three-person group, but nobody volunteered. It was embarrassing. There was Pamela standing alone while Mr. Eshenko tried to find her a group.

"Marissa, Jennifer?" he asked. "I'm sure Pamela could help you."

"We'd rather not, Mr. E.," Marissa said. "Pamela and I don't get along very well."

Pamela tried to pretend that it didn't bother her. But, by the way her smile was trembling, I could tell it did. In a way, I didn't like it, but if she was going to be rude, then this stuff was going to happen.

Finally, she got control of her face and mumbled, "That's fine with me. I'd rather do a monologue anyway."

Chris and I pretended to work on a funny skit, but we were really discussing our problem. We drew a complete blank on another *great idea* to extract ourselves from the depth of the mess. "There's only one thing to do," Chris declared as we walked home from school.

"What's that?"

"When all else fails, speak to Reese. Come by my house after supper and we'll ask my brother what to do."

I didn't have much of an appetite for dinner. Twice, Mom reached across the table to feel my forehead. "You usually like my southern fried chicken," she said in her concerned-parent voice.

"I'm not sick, Mom. I'm just not very hungry tonight, that's all."

"Can I have your chicken then, Jordy?" Alison asked.

I handed her a drumstick.

Mom cut a biscuit and buttered it. "Jordy," she said, "our school secretary is Olive Boyer and she has a boy at Kennedy Junior High. He's in seventh grade."

"Oh, yeah," I said absently.

"His name is Clarence. Do you know him?"

"No," I said. Then I remembered the overweight kid who'd wished me luck Monday morning. "I mean yes. I met him once."

"Well," Mom continued, "Mrs. Boyer told me that her son is really excited about a skateboard contest this Saturday. Do you know anything about it?"

She immediately had my full attention. I tried to act as calm as possible and ate another forkful of mashed potatoes before answering. "I heard some of the kids talking about it," I said casually.

"Mrs. Boyer also said something curious. She said that there was a big bet going on between one of the seventh grade boys and a ninth grade boy. And she thinks that the boy in seventh grade is called Jordy Shepherd."

"She thinks that?"

Mom nodded. "I told her that there must be another Jordy Shepherd because you don't even own a skateboard. I told her that my Jordy knows exactly how I feel about skateboarding and he would never enter a contest like that." Then she looked directly into my eyes. "Is there another boy called Jordy Shepherd in your class?"

I speared more potatoes, but figured I'd never get them down my dry throat. "No," I told her.

"Then you're the Jordy Shepherd she's talking about?" my mother said in her surprised-parent voice.

"Yes," I said.

She placed the butter knife carefully on her plate. "Then you had better do some fast explaining, young man."

Young man? That was the phrase my mother reserved for the times when I do something that really upsets her. She'd only used it a couple of times before, both in Great Falls . . . when I skipped out of school to go bike-riding with friends and when I forgot that she was going to be late and went to the mall instead of baby-sitting Alison.

"Well," she insisted. "I'm waiting."

And I almost told her the truth. Except for regular white fibs, such as not telling her I'd spent my whole allowance on video games, I'd never lied to my mom before. Never about anything serious. And right then, I wanted to tell her the truth. I wanted to dump this whole problem on her lap. But something stopped me.

I'm not sure if it was because I was afraid of her disappointment. Or if I was concerned how the kids at school would react when they discovered *my mother* wouldn't let me have a skateboard. Or it could have been my worry about Chris's reaction; he'd lose his money for sure. And certainly there was Marissa to think of. Perhaps all of those reasons influenced what I said next.

"Mrs. Boyer has things mixed-up." I made a chuckle that didn't sound all that convincing. "There is a skateboard competition this Saturday, but I don't have anything to do with it. We're doing comedy sketches in English class. Chris and I are doing one about a couple of boys who have a bet with each other."

Her face relaxed. "This contest talk is just a school assignment?"

"Right," I nodded.

"And it doesn't have anything to do with skateboarding?"

"Nothing."

She let out a long breath and then made a nervous chuckle as well. "For a moment, I thought . . ." she concluded in her relieved-parent voice.

"Things can get mixed-up," I said.

"I guess you think I'm being silly about skateboarding. You must think it odd that I got so upset. Especially now that you're in seventh grade."

Now that she'd mentioned it, I did think that her feelings about skateboards were extreme. "It seems that every kid in Flower Valley has one," I pointed out the obvious.

"I may be overly cautious and protective, but I've seen so many children . . ."

"Hurt themselves," I finished for her. "I know, I've heard it before. More than once."

"Jordy!" she snapped. "I don't like your tone of voice."

"And I don't deserve the lecture," I snapped back. "You're right. I am in seventh grade."

"Are you telling me that you want a skateboard?"

We weren't even close to the same wavelength. She was thinking I was upset because I wanted a bloody skateboard. I wished the things didn't exist.

"No," I grumbled. "I don't want a board."

"Do you blame me for not letting you have one?"

Wasn't that the same question? I wanted to say that I blamed her for not letting me have a board in fourth grade. If I'd had one for three years, then maybe I'd have a chance of beating Steve Powell and going out with his sister.

"Then you have no reason to be angry with me," she reasoned.

"Let's just forget it," I suggested.

"That's fine with me, Jordy. You know, sometimes it's hard for me to turn off being a teacher. Sometimes I forget that my little boy isn't so little anymore. Let's not argue. I hate it when we're upset with each other."

"O.K., Mom. I got to go over to Chris's place now. Just leave the plates, I'll do the dishwasher later, all right?"

"Are you going to practice your comedy skit?"

"Right now it isn't all that funny," I told her. It wouldn't hurt to tell her one true fact.

Chapter Eleven

You Have Two Choices

As I was walking down our driveway, Alison called to me, "Jordy, Jordy."

I stopped and waited for her.

"I'm gonna be in bed when you get home," she said. "I want to tell you now what happened with my problem."

"Rotten Roger," I nodded. "How's the booger king?"

"Well, I did just like you told me. We were doing seat work and I leaned across and said, 'Roger, I'd like to be your friend.' "

"What did he say?"

"He made a funny noise, kind of like a glurf."

"A glurf?"

"Kind of. I can't do it. Then he started rolling his eyes and dribbling," she went on. "So I said it again, 'Roger, I'd like to be your friend.' "

"What did he say this time?"

"Nothing. He stuck his head in his desk."

"His whole head?" I asked.

"Up to his shoulders," she said. "Right in there with his books and crayons."

"And then what?"

"Then he started pushing on his desk with his hands. He was stuck."

I started to smile. "Roger got his head caught in his desk?"

"Ms. Dudley looked back and I guess she couldn't see Roger. So she asked where he was. I told her that he was still in his seat. It was just that his head was stuck in his desk."

I started to laugh. "Ms. Dudley must have broken up."

"Oh, no," Alison said seriously. "She was really upset because the principal was coming to make a classroom visit."

"The principal was coming to check on her and old Roger was pulling an ostrich with his desk? That's great." I laughed. "Thanks for cheering me up. You don't know how much I needed this."

"The principal had to get the caretaker to unscrew the desk. Roger was crying."

I wiped tears from my eyes. "I wish I could have seen it. You know, there's been times in the past couple of days when I think it would have been a good idea to get my head stuck in a desk."

"Then it's normal for boys to do that?"

"For some of us anyway."

I gave Alison a kiss and cut through a couple of backyards to Chris's place. He was sitting on the front steps waiting for me. "Hi, Jordy. Come on in. Reese is up in his room. I've told him everything."

We went inside and up the stairs. Chris knocked on his brother's door.

"Enter."

Reese was sitting on his desk with his feet resting on his chair. He was casually spinning a football in his hands.

"Hi, Jordy," he said, smiling. He was wearing gym shorts and a basketball t-shirt which showed off his muscles. Guys like me could pump iron for a decade and only look half as good.

As Chris had told me when we first met, Reese has a lot of things going for him. It isn't just his muscles, it's everything. His tan, the shoulder-length sandy hair, the silver earring, the dark eyes. Everything. But it's not just the way he looks. He seems in control and on top of things. He makes you want to be around him. My mother says he has *charisma*.

Reese told us to sit on the edge of the bed.

"I've heard all about your problem," Reese said. "It just goes to show that if you lie once, you have to keep on lying. Things get worse. You've both been stupid."

"We know we've been stupid," Chris agreed. "But we're up against the wall now. We can't back out without looking like utter jerks."

Reese nodded. "And Steve would want his two hundred. And he'd probably still pound on both of you."

"You'd stop him, huh?" Chris asked.

His brother shook his head. "There's a moral lesson in this. You made the mess; you're going to have to solve it."

"Stop sounding like Mary Poppins and help us," Chris pleaded.

"I'll give you advice, but that's all."

"So what can we do?" I asked.

"You've got two choices," Reese began. "And only two. Unless you want to bust your leg for real or move back to Montana?"

"Both of those sound attractive to me at this point," I told him.

"But not practical," Reese continued. "Here's what is. First, you can go the honesty route."

"What?" Chris gasped.

"The disadvantages are: everyone will think you're stupid, you end up losing two hundred."

"This isn't a choice," Chris protested.

"You'd have to work out some kind of payment schedule with Steve. Pay him back out of your route money," he said to his brother. "And you'd lose your rep and your girlfriend," he said to me. "Plus you both get a boot to the head from Steve."

"That doesn't help us any," Chris said.

"The advantage of 'fessing up is that it's all over with," Reese pointed out. "You take your medicine and get on with your lives. And you feel good because you've told the truth."

"What if we don't want to feel good?" Chris asked. "What's the other choice?"

Reese placed the football down and folded his hands on his knees. "Well, I don't really like to suggest that you lie once more. But since you both seem upset by this, and since you've both learned your lesson . . ."

"Yeah, yeah, we have," Chris said impatiently.

"And since we're family," Reese gave his brother a stern look. "I suggest that the injury idea was a good one. You just tried to fake it at the wrong time."

"What do you mean?" Chris and I asked together.

"You fake it on Saturday during the contest."

"Get real, Reese," Chris said.

"I've never been on a skateboard in my life," I added.

"I know that," Reese explained. "But you've got to get on a skateboard Saturday afternoon and start a routine."

"Everyone will laugh at him," Chris said.

"No," Reese shook his head. "It doesn't get to

that point. Jordy just *starts* a routine. He learns a few basic moves, a fakie, a one-eighty. Then he tries a hard stunt. He wipes out, fakes an injury, and it's all over. Everyone will have seen Jordy try, but because he got hurt, Steve can't say that he won.''

"That's terrific!" Chris said. "I love it. It's great! We should have thought of that.''

"Wait a minute," I said. "You're both forgetting something. I've never been on a skateboard. Ever. I don't think I can learn even the basic moves in the next three days. And if I fake an accident, I'd probably end up really hurting myself.''

"Not if you've got the right teacher," Reese explained.

"Of course," Chris grinned. "I can teach you the basics.''

"No, not you," Reese said. "We need the best. Someone who can show him how to fall.''

"You going to teach him yourself?" Chris wondered.

"Not me." Reese smiled. "The best. We need Pamela Loseth.''

Chapter Twelve

The Best Skate-Betty

"Pamela Loseth! Pam-e-la Lo-seth. That's terrific, Reese." Chris sounded like a machine gun of chuckles. "That's really funny."

Reese watched his brother. He wasn't smiling.

"Pam-e-la Lo-seth," Chris continued to roll. "Can you picture Pamela on a skateboard? I can just see it. What a hoot." He slipped off the bed onto the floor.

"You're not kidding?" I asked Reese.

He shook his head slowly.

Chris was clutching his stomach. "Oh, I can't stand it. I've got to stop. If I don't stop laughing, I'm going to chuck."

"Really, you're not joking?" I asked again.

Once more, Reese shook his head.

" 'We need Pamela Loseth,' " Chris mimicked. He banged the floor. "Oh, stop, stop."

I leaned over the edge of the bed. "He's not kidding."

" 'Pamela, please show me how to grab air,' " Chris needed three breaths to finish the sentence.

"Reese means it," I called down.

"Reese means it," Chris echoed.

"Reese means it," I repeated.

"Reese means it," he laughed.

"Pamela Loseth can skate?" I asked.

"The best skate-betty I've seen," Reese said.

"A skate-betty is a girl who's good on a skate-board?"

Reese nodded. "She's the best."

"Reese means it?!" Chris sat up and stared at his brother. "You're putting us on? Pamela's no thrasher. I've never seen her with a board."

"I have," Reese smiled. "I was cutting through the park late one night in August. I heard the sound of wheels on the skateboard ramp. We're not talking the sound of fakies. We're talking side air, back air, hand plants, the works. So I went over to watch the dude. Turns out I'm looking at a thirteen-year-old girl by the name of Pamela Loseth."

"No . . ." Chris said in disbelief.

"The one and only."

Chris climbed back on the bed. "Come on, Reese. Pamela Loseth couldn't do that."

"Why not?"

" 'Cause, I've never seen her with a board, that's why. She's never entered any competitions," Chris said. "If she was hot stuff, she'd strut it. We'd all know."

Reese began to drum on his knees. Then he arched his eyebrows.

"What's that mean?" I asked.

"It means that Pamela Loseth marches to a different beat," Reese explained. "She lives right across from the park, right? She told me that she waits until everyone goes home, then she uses the ramp."

"You're making this up," Chris said.

"Not at all," Reese went on. "I asked why she wasn't grandstanding her talent. You know what she said?"

"What?" Chris and I muttered together.

"Pamela told me that she left that kind of stuff to

the coneheads. She said that there was no reason to show off. As I said, the girl is in tune to a different step. But," Reese paused and grabbed the football again, "she's the only person I know who can show you how to wipe without breaking your neck."

"Whoa," Chris said. "Let's suppose that you're not guffing us. Suppose that Pamela Loseth *is* the greatest thing to come along since Cherry 7-Up. Why her? There are other people in Flower Valley who can grab air. You can. So can your friends, Rich and Anwar. Why Pamela Loseth?

"Because she's the only other person who knows that Jordy is posing. She's already keeping your secret. She's the natural person to ask for help."

"I believe you, Reese," I told him. "I don't see why you'd make all this up. But we can't ask Pamela for help."

"Why not?"

"Because she doesn't like me. She calls me Dopey. In fact, she doesn't like anybody. I can't see her wanting to help out."

"Then you're wrong," Reese declared. "I happen to know she'll help you."

"How do you know that?" Chris wondered.

"Because she told me. Whose plan do you think this is anyway?"

"You're saying that Pamela Loseth gave you this idea?" I asked.

"That's right. Apparently, she was going to suggest it to you in school the other day, Jordy. But you stomped off."

"Yesterday, at lunch," I remembered. "She asked me if I wanted some advice. That means she must have known I was in trouble."

"That's what she told me on the phone tonight."

Reese began to smile. "She called me because she figured that you'd come to me for help. I think her words were, 'Even if you add their I.Q.'s together, you'd still have a single number.' "

"Why, that . . ." Chris complained.

Reese looked right at me. "Then she told me that you were too much of a gomer to be a thrasher. She said that it was obvious that Chris's big mouth and your starry-eyes for Marissa Powell had landed you neck deep. But she told me that she was willing to help you. And then she told me the plan."

Chris was shaking his head. "This is ultra-weird. I can't see Pamela doing that. She's not that nice a person."

"She does have a price," Reese pointed out.

"A price?" I said. "What does she want? How much money?"

"She didn't tell me. But I don't think it's money. She said, 'If Jordy does a favor for me, I'll do this for him.' Why don't you go over and talk to her right now. She said that she'd be expecting you for your first lesson tonight."

Chapter Thirteen

Do We Have a Deal?

"Best of luck, good buddy." Chris slapped my shoulder. "Remember to call me as soon as you get home. It doesn't matter how late it is. I want to hear how you make out with her."

I looked at the stuccoed two-story home of Pamela Loseth. Then I glanced across the road at the park. I searched the semi-darkness for the ramp, not quite sure of what I was looking for. The only things that the street lamps revealed were trees and a couple of benches.

"I have to do this, right?"

"Reese's advice," Chris said. "I wonder what her price is?"

"I'll find out shortly, won't I?"

"Maybe she'll want you to kiss her." He chuckled. "Bet she's never been kissed by a boy before. Or maybe she'll want you to take her to the Halloween dance."

"I'll see you later," I said as I walked up the front path.

"Phone me," he called.

I have to do this, I said to myself. *I have to do this so the kids won't think I'm a geek. This way will guarantee that Marissa and I will be going together. Chris will keep his money. Everything will work out.*

There wasn't a bell, just an old-looking brass

knocker in the middle of the door. I rapped it a couple of times.

A few seconds later, the door opened and an attractive lady greeted me. I had no trouble telling it was Pamela's mother. Her hair, although flecked with grey, was definitely the same red.

"Hello, I'm . . ." I began.

". . . Jordy Shepherd." Doctor Loseth smiled. "Of course. I've heard a lot about you in the past few weeks. Pamela has talked about you since the first day of school."

I could imagine the things she'd said. The cowboy. Dopey. The poser. The gomer.

"Oh yes," Doctor Loseth continued as she invited me in. "And let me say that you are indeed as handsome as my daughter declared. I know she's looking forward to you coming over."

"Huh?"

"Pamela!" she called. "Jordy is here."

Pamela thumped down the stairs. She was wearing cut-off yellow jeans, with an old, black AC/DC t-shirt. Add her red Keds and the purple glasses and she was a walking color clash.

"Hey." She nodded at me. "We'll be in the garage and driveway, Mom. I got to teach Jordy a few tricks."

"Fine, dear," Doctor Loseth said. "Let me know if you go to the ramp."

"Sure thing. Let's go, Dopey."

"Dopey?" her mother wondered.

"His nickname," Pamela offered in way of explanation. "Let's go."

We walked down the hall, through the kitchen and into the empty double garage. "I told Mom to park on the street," Pamela told me as she flicked the light.

"You know, it really bugs me to be called Dopey. You're insulting me."

"But it fits, doesn't it?" She grinned. "I mean, you're here, where you don't want to be, because you were a dope."

"I want you to stop it. You wouldn't like it if I went around insulting you all the time?"

"It wouldn't bother me." She took a skateboard off a shelf. "I'm used to it. Don't you listen? What's your girlfriend call me?"

"It doesn't matter what anybody else does," I pointed out. "It matters what I do. I don't insult you, so I don't expect it from you."

She nodded. "Fair enough. Maybe you *don't* deserve it."

"Thanks."

"But it sure fits," she added. "I guess Reese told you about my plan. Just the fact that you're here means that you think it's a good idea."

"I don't see that I have much choice. This seems the only way out."

"Yeah, that's what I figured. And you can trust me, Dope . . . Jordy. I can teach you how to pull a wipe that will have everyone believing you hurt yourself. And I'll keep my mouth shut too."

"You know, I didn't think you would be the type of person who'd be willing to help. I mean, you haven't been exactly friendly to me."

"I'm not doing this for friendship. Didn't Reese tell you that I wanted a return of favor?"

Pamela held the skateboard in front of her and dropped it. Before it hit the ground, she was standing on it.

"What do you want?"

"Not much. I want you to be my partner for the comedy skits that Mr. Eshenko assigned today in English class."

"Your partner? But I'm already working with Chris."

"He'll understand, won't he?" She pushed on the back of her board and placed her other foot on the front. Then she twisted around in a circle.

"Why would you want me to be your partner?"

"I've got my reasons," she said.

She stomped heavily on the back of her skateboard. It flipped into the air and she grabbed it by the front wheels.

"It's Marissa, isn't it? You want me to be your partner so that Marissa Powell will get upset. You're mad at her because of what she said in class today. You want to get back at her."

Pamela shrugged. "I got my reasons," she repeated.

"That's not fair, Pamela," I told her. "You're using me."

"And you're not using me?" she asked. "You're here because I can do something for you. Well, fair trade. You want that, then you do something for me."

"What am I going to tell Marissa?"

She snorted a laugh. "You'll figure something. It won't take anything elaborate. Miss Bubblebrain isn't too rich with the grey matter."

"Why do you do that? Why do you insult people?"

"Do we have a deal or not?" she asked impatiently.

"Like I said before, I don't have much choice, do I?"

There's always a choice, D . . . Jordy."

"We have a deal," I said.

"Good." She smiled. "Now let me teach you how to use a skateboard."

Chapter Fourteen

Why, What, and Bug Off

"That's an elbow pad," Pamela told me. "That's why you can't get it past your ankle. The big ones are the knee pads."

I slipped the pad off and pulled it up my arm. "These things don't give me much confidence," I told her. "It reminds me that I'm going to fall off."

She pulled a helmet from the shelf and tossed it to me. "Everybody falls off once in a while. The pads mean that you won't hurt yourself." She paused for a moment. "As much."

She held the board in front of her. "How many times have you used a board before?" she asked. "Where do we have to start?"

I put my thumb and index finger together to indicate a zero.

"Really?" she said.

I thought she'd be more surprised. In fact, I half-expected her to say that since I was a complete novice, she couldn't teach me anything in three days. But she just bit her bottom lip and nodded. "Then we'd better get busy. Let me introduce you to a skateboard."

Five minutes later, I knew what a baseplate was. I'd also learned how to identify a truck, a hanger, a kingpin and a tail skid.

"Now this board is for ramp work," Pamela explained. "The wheels are hard. I like that on a ramp. If you're doing a lot of street stuff, then you usually get softer wheels."

If you say so, I thought.

"The flat part of the skateboard, the part you stand on, is called the deck. On this board it's laminated wood, seven layers thick. You notice how large it is, wider than street boards?"

"I wouldn't really know," I confessed.

"Well, that's because a wider deck makes the ramp stunts a little easier." She placed the board on the cement floor of the garage. "Watch how I get on. If you don't do it right, you're going to end up on your butt."

I watched her and then I tried it and I ended up on my rear end anyway. She ha-horked a few times. "Those little wheels just want to go, don't they?" She helped me up. "I did that the first time as well. Try it again."

For the next hour and a half, Pamela showed me how to feel comfortable on a skateboard. She taught me how to place my resting foot to get balance, how to shift the weight on my power foot to get smooth acceleration, how to cruise with feet in line and angled, and how to lean into turns both wide and sharp.

By the time we were finished, I'd only wiped out about thirty-six times. My thighs were aching from the exercise.

"Not bad," Pamela said. "Not bad at all. Considering you were a greener, you've done pretty good."

I pulled off the pads. "Everything inside of me feels bruised," I complained.

"Part of learning how to fly. Just remember what I told you. If you feel that you're losing it, jump off."

"Thanks for being so patient," I said. "You're a good teacher."

"Tomorrow, we'll do more of the same. When you start to feel that the board belongs under your feet, then we try the ramp. Now let's go inside and work on the comedy skit."

"You're different," I told her. "Ever since we started on the board, you've been different. You haven't insulted me. You haven't made a stupid comment. How come?"

I thought that perhaps we could begin a half-intelligent conversation. Instead I got cut off. "Look, Jordy, I was doing my part of the deal. Now's the time to do yours."

"Fine." I pitched the pads onto the shelf. "Let me do my part so that I can get out of here."

I followed her into the kitchen. "You thirsty?" she asked. "We got pop, juice, water."

I ended up with a glass of apple juice.

"Now, I've been thinking of this skit and I've got a few ideas," she told me. "You remember the Abbott and Costello routine about 'Who's on first?' You know, where the first base guy is called Who?"

"Yeah, it's funny."

"Well, why don't we try something like that? Use that routine, but make it something about school."

I took a long swallow of juice. "It could be O.K., I guess. What do you have in mind?"

"I was thinking that I'd dress up as this really dignified lady, Miss Bompas. Miss Bompas is head of the school board. We'll make believe that she's visiting the school to watch a band concert. You dress up in something way out. Punk, maybe. You can be one of the students watching the same concert. Now just to get us going, let's call the trumpet player, *Why*.

What is playing saxophone and . . ." She paused to think. *"Bug Off* is on the drums. You got that?"

I nodded. *"Why* is on trumpet, *What* is on sax and *Bug Off* is the drummer."

"Right. Let's try it." She arranged two chairs side by side and motioned me to sit down. "O.K., you're the student watching the concert and I come and sit beside you."

"We can tape a band practice and have it playing," I suggested.

"Good idea," she agreed. "But it would have to be soft, so the class could hear us."

"I'll give you a funny look when you sit down."

"And I'll look down my nose at you," she went on. She raised the pitch of her voice and started to talk like a stuck-up person. "This band is very good, isn't it?"

"Ugh," I grunted.

She ha-horked. "Great touch." Then she went back into her dignified lady mode. "I say, who is that wonderful trumpet player?"

"Why."

"Because I want to know. Who is he?"

"Why."

"Because I'm interested. What is his name?"

"No. *What* is playing sax."

She leaned forward as if she was studying the make-believe band. "There is a girl playing the saxophone."

"Right," I said. *"What."*

She pretended to be frustrated. "A girl is playing the saxophone. I don't want to know *her* name. I want to know the name of the boy with the trumpet?"

"Why."

"Arrgh. I want to know because I want to know. What is his name?"

I shook my head. "No. *What* is her name. On the sax."

"How am I supposed to know that?"

"Look, lady. That's her name."

"What?"

"That's right."

"What?"

"Right. And that's *Why* on trumpet."

"What's why?"

"How did you know they were going out?"

"Who is going out?"

"What and *Why."*

Pamela grabbed her forehead as if she was deeply frustrated. "All right, let me try this one last time. What is the name of the trumpet player?"

"No, *What* is the name of the girl on the saxophone."

"I don't know. Why?"

"He's on the trumpet."

"Fine! Forget the name of the trumpet player. Just tell me who is playing the drums?"

"Bug Off." I smiled.

She turned to me and started to laugh. Ha-hork. Ha-hork.

And I was laughing just as hard.

"That wasn't bad at all," she said. "In fact, it was pretty funny. Especially when you picked up on 'What's why.' "

"I like it," I agreed. "We make a pretty good team."

"What are you two laughing at?" Doctor Loseth poked her head into the kitchen. "What's so funny?"

"She sure is," I chuckled.

"Why are you laughing?" her mom repeated.

"We don't know," Pamela said. "I guess you'll have to ask him."

That sent us off again. Pamela's mother regarded us for a few moments, shook her head and left us alone.

"You're funny, Pamela," I told her after I caught my breath. "And you're different again."

She looked at me, seemed about to say something, and turned away. "I'll see you at school tomorrow," she said.

When I got home, I called Chris from the downstairs phone so that my mother wouldn't hear me. I filled him in on my skateboard progress and told him about Pamela's price. He didn't object to losing me as a comedy partner. In fact, he thought it was cheap way to return the favor. I promised to help him write a monologue.

"I'm glad to hear this stuff, Jordy," he said. "This makes me feel a whole lot better."

"Say, Chris, before you hang up. Tell me about Pamela. How long you known her?"

"I don't know. Second grade. Maybe third grade. Why?"

"Has she always been . . . strange?"

"Always. Fruit and nut bar."

"You ever talk to her? I mean really talk."

"No. Why?"

I just wondered, that's all."

"Why?"

"He's the trumpet player," I said.

"Pardon."

"Good night, Chris."

Chapter Fifteen

Great Sport

On Wednesday morning a large group of seventh graders were waiting for me by the front doors. They'd painted a long banner which said "Jumpin' Jordy Flash—Major Thrasher." When I got closer they started to chant and cheer.

When Marissa saw me, she ran over and kissed my cheek. "Just so the other girls don't get any ideas," she whispered.

I thanked everyone for the welcome and then politely requested that they make less fuss about the contest. That was shouted down with cries of "Jumpin' Jordy" and "Seventh Grade Rules."

It then dawned on me that, come Saturday, there were going to be a lot of disappointed people . . . from my classmates to my teachers. This thing had become an event and I was going to let everyone down. I wished it was next week already. I wanted the whole thing to be finished, over with.

Mr. Eshenko was delighted when I told him that Pamela and I were going to work on a comedy skit together and Chris was going to do a monologue. Mr. E.'s enthusiasm was equaled by Marissa's outrage.

She steered me to a corner table at lunch so we could be alone. "Why, Jordy? Why?"

"I owe Pamela for something. It doesn't have anything to do with you, Marissa. I'm doing her a favor.''

"It doesn't have anything to do with me?'' she said in disbelief. "For the past three days, everyone thinks that you and I are getting close. Now you're doing an English assignment with *her.*''

"That's all it is. It's just an assignment,'' I explained. "It doesn't mean Pamela and I are engaged or anything.''

"I don't mean that,'' Marissa hissed. "Everybody knows that you wouldn't go out with her. Especially when I'm around. But it makes me look bad anyway.''

"How do you figure that?''

"Because one of my friends, you, is doing an assignment with a piece of scum, her,'' she reasoned.

"That doesn't make any sense, Marissa. And I don't think that Pamela deserves to be called that.''

She arched her back and glared at me. "Why are you sticking up for her?''

"This whole conversation is silly,'' I said.

"Silly? Well, I'll tell you what's silly.'' Little pieces of spit misted into the air. "You *do* want us to go together, don't you?''

"Yeah, I'd like that,'' I told her.

"Well, there's no way it'll happen if you do your assignment with Pamela on Monday. I don't care what happens on Saturday. If you work with her, then you and I are a no-show. Do you understand?''

"Marissa, do you know what you're saying?''

"How's *that* for silly!'' she snarled as she stood up and stomped toward her friends' table. I hoped she'd change her mind after Monday, but right now I needed Pamela more than I needed Marissa.

After school, Mom gave me the money to take Alison to McDonald's. "I have to go back to my class-room for about an hour to put up a display for parent interview day tomorrow. I'll be back by seven."

"I have to go visit somebody tonight," I told her. "So I can't baby-sit."

"I said, I'll be back by seven. Who are you going to visit?"

"A girl," I told her. "Pamela Loseth. She's in my English class. We're doing an assignment together." *Tell as much truth as possible,* I thought. "Doctor Loseth is her mom."

"Oh." Mom winked at me. "Visiting a *girl.*"

"It's for school," I said.

"I see." She winked at me again.

Alison and I rode our bikes to McDonald's.

"Roger spoke to me today," she told me as she finished her chocolate sundae.

"He did? Hey, a breakthrough. What did old Roger say?"

"He came up to me at recess and asked if I wanted part of his Mars bar."

"Well," I said, smiling, "that is truly a civilized and friendly gesture."

"I said that would be nice."

"Ah," I sighed. "This sounds like the beginning of a long friendship, Alison."

"Then he said I couldn't have any," she went on. "And he ate the whole thing himself."

"The gorf. Maybe my advice about making friends wasn't all that hot. Maybe you should ignore him completely."

"He ate everything, the wrapper and everything."

"He ate the wrapper?"

"Everything. Maybe I'll ask him if he wants to come for supper one night. Mom said that we can invite people for supper if we tell her ahead. Maybe that'll make him my friend and he won't act so dumb."

"Somehow I don't think that would be a good move. This boy sounds terminally stupid to me," I told her as I looked at my watch. "Let's get going. Mom should be back by now. I've got to go practice something."

It was dark by the time I got to Pamela's house. "You're late," she said as she opened her door.

"My mother's fault," I told her. "She had to go back to school and I was baby-sitting my sister."

We went into the garage and suited up in pads and helmets. "Do you think we're going to be able to do this?" I asked. "Do you think that you can teach me enough to be convincing on Saturday?"

She nodded. "No doubt about it. If I didn't, then I wouldn't be wasting my time."

"What do we do first?"

"First, you tell me what Marissa said to you at lunch. She looked like she was really chewing you out."

"That's what you wanted, wasn't it?" I asked.

"You bet." She grinned. "Bubblebrain blows up. Great sport."

"Then you got what you wanted."

"What did she say? Exactly?"

"A few unflattering things about you."

She ha-horked.

"And that if I did the skit with you on Monday, then she wouldn't be friends with me anymore."

"All right!" Pamela smacked her hands together. "She was that mad? All right!"

"Really does me a lot of good, doesn't it?" I said.

78

Pamela stared at me. "I . . . I . . . All right! She was really mad."

"Thanks for the sympathy," I said sarcastically.

She took the skateboard off the shelf, placed it on the floor and kicked it toward me.

"Let's get busy," she said.

I placed my left foot on the board, I pushed off, and steered the skateboard in a circle around her.

Pamela opened the garage door. "I want you to go down the driveway, turn and stop on the sidewalk. If you think you can't stop, jump off the board. I don't want to scrape you off the road."

I sweep-pushed with my leg, angled my feet on the board, bent my knees and quickly picked up speed. As I was sailing on the asphalt with the cool evening air blowing through the helmet, I felt good. For the last five days, I'd felt awful—worried, anxious, depressed. Now as the ball bearings and wheels hummed and the board swayed gently as I adjusted my balance, I actually felt good.

So this is what it's about, I thought. *This is what's so great about these things*.

I let out a small whoop as the board hit the sidewalk. I made a tight left turn and then shifted my weight to the back. As the front of the board rose, I lifted my right foot, the tail skid scraped along the pavement, and I made a perfect stop.

"Who taught you that move?" Pamela wanted to know. "How'd you learn that?"

"I watched you," I told her.

She punched my arm. "I'm impressed. Now do it again."

So I did it a second time. And a third. And a fifth. And a fifteenth. "I'm getting tired of this," I complained. "When can we go to the ramp?"

"Soon. Do it one more time."

I pushed up her driveway for my sixteenth run. This time I went right to the back of the garage and began with three leg sweeps. By the time I cleared the door, I was flying. I crouched low and the board went even faster. The air was whistling inside the helmet.

Pamela was standing on the sidewalk smiling at me. She reached into her pocket and held out her hand so that I could see what she'd retrieved. Silver nails reflected the street light. Casually, she tossed them onto the driveway, right in front of the skateboard.

Chapter Sixteen

Just Showing Off

I didn't have any time to think and barely enough time to react. I stood up, shifted weight and dropped the tail skid. I slowed, but not enough to miss the nails. The rear wheels hit the metal and jammed. The board stopped and I kept going. Fortunately, at the instant the skateboard froze, I was jumping. I landed off-balance, danced crazily on the sidewalk for a few moments and then stumbled onto my knee pads.

It took me only seconds to get to my feet and shout a string of suitable words into Pamela's face.

"That was a smooth move," she interrupted. *"Now* you're ready for the ramp. I'm going to go over and check that no one's there. I mean, it won't do for someone to see you using it for the first time, will it?"

As my anger wore off, I began to feel proud. I had handled the nails well. It was my second day on a board and I was doing good. No, I was doing great.

I picked up Pamela's skateboard and tucked it under my arm, the way Steve Powell did. Now I was posing, but I knew that I wasn't just a poser anymore. A car went by and honked. I could see some kids in the back seat waving to me, but I couldn't see who they were. I made a casual salute as the car drove down the street.

Pamela jogged across the road from the park. "All

clear. I'll tell my mom and then we'll go take out a ramp."

We walked to the center of the park. The path ended in a flat area that was surrounded on all sides by slight hills. *That's why I couldn't see anything from Pamela's street,* I thought.

What I could see now was a small playground, a softball diamond, and a U-shaped structure of painted plywood and two by fours. The middle of the U was at chest height and stretched about twenty-four feet across. It was about half that wide and half again high.

"What's this?" I asked.

"The ramp," she told me.

"The ramp? This isn't a ramp. A ramp is a little, slopey thing."

"This is a half-pipe ramp," she affirmed.

"How can you skateboard in that?" I wondered. "It looks like a big, flat U."

"I guess that's a fair way to describe it," she agreed. "And to answer your question, we climb up to the top of the U and drop in."

"Drop in?"

"Take the board to the edge and just push over the side."

"Push over the side?"

"What's the matter? Aren't I speaking in English?"

"How do you drop into something that's six feet high?"

"Eight feet," she corrected.

"Eight feet!"

"It's not that hard," she assured me. "But don't worry about it right now. First, get used to skating inside. We'll drop in tomorrow."

We climbed the stairs at the back of the ramp and stood on the top platform. Pamela took the board from me and placed the front wheels on the plastic tubing on the edge of the U.

"The edge is called the lip. The plastic tube that covers it is the grind," she told me. Then she simply rolled forward and dropped into the ramp.

I expected to hear the crunch of girl and skateboard. Instead, I saw her sailing up the other vertical side of the U. She let the board stop and slid backwards into the center. "It's really not that hard. Not much different from going down my driveway," she shouted.

She rolled up next to me, stopped and went down backwards again. "This is called a fakie. Easy stuff." As she rode the opposite wall she leaned and turned the skateboard so that it was going down frontwards. "A one-eighty," she yelled. "I'll have you doing these tonight."

She did several more one-eighties, each time gathering more speed as she tore from wall to wall. I thought that if she went any faster the board was going to fly over the lip and into mid-air.

And it did.

Pamela and the board took off, at least a yard above the lip. As she went airborne, she reached down and grabbed the board and twisted it under her feet. When she fell, she pushed the wheels back against the wall.

"Grabbing air," she called. And she repeated the move a few more times showing me "Side air!" and "Back air!"

Then she grabbed air and grabbed the lip with her free hand. "Hand plant," she told me.

Finally she grabbed air, but instead of dropping down into the ramp, she landed with a vicious thud on the lip. The trucks rested on the plastic tubing, one wheel on each side. "And that's called a body-jar," she finished. "For obvious reasons."

I shook my head slowly. "I'll never be able to do that. Never."

"I was showing off, Jordy. On Saturday, you'll do a fakie and a one-eighty, then I'll show you how to fake a slam."

"A slam?"

"A wipe-out." She let the board drop into the U. "Climb down and start pushing off. Let the board coast up and fall back."

"A fakie," I said as I sat on the lip and eased myself down into the U.

And to my surprise, it wasn't as tough as I thought. I wiped out a fair number of times, but within a half hour, I'd pulled a few decent one-eighties. Pamela cheered me on, told me I was a natural a couple of times. I was disappointed when we had to stop.

"I have to go home now," Pamela said.

We walked back to her house and practiced our skit again. By the time we were in her garage, we were both laughing. I felt so good, tired and happy at the same time.

As I took off the pads and helmet and placed them on the shelf, I watched Pamela. Her glasses slipped off as she laughed at the "Bug off" line.

Pamela's laughter was infectious. It sounded stupid, the way she snorked between each ha-ha, but it sure sounded like she was having fun. In a way, it was sort of . . . cute.

She brushed her long-hair side back over the short-hair side and grinned at me the same way Alison does on Christmas morning. Without her silly, purple glasses, with the wide smile, she was definitely . . . cute.

"You want a Coke or something?" she asked.

"No thanks. I should go before my mom starts to worry."

She nodded. "We had fun, huh?"

"It was an interesting evening," I agreed.

"Look, Jordy, I've been thinking, about the skit. You don't have to do it with me."

"Pardon?" I picked up her glasses and handed them to her.

"You don't have to work with me. I don't want Marissa to give you a hard time."

"But I thought that you wanted to get her mad."

"I did, but that wasn't the only reason; I wanted to work with you. I really did want to work with *you.*"

"You wanted . . . Pamela, this is tough for me to understand. I mean, you're being different again. It's like the person you are at school isn't the same girl I'm talking to now."

"That's because I feel O.K. around you."

"I've really enjoyed being with you the past couple of days," I told her. "How come you're not like this with the other kids? How come you don't feel O.K. around them?"

She didn't say anything for several seconds, as if she was deciding whether she wanted to talk or not. "Because most of the time, they bug me," she complained. "Ever since I was a little kid, they've given me a hard time. So I return it. You must have noticed I'm a little strange. I got a funny laugh. I tend to be a might outspoken."

"You mean like, 'Did Dopey die?' " I said.

"I feel bad about that now," she smiled. "Kind of. It got your attention, didn't it?"

"But don't you think the kids are giving you a hard time because you're acting like a . . ."

"Weirdo?" she finished for me. "They think I am anyway."

"But I wonder what came first, you know, the chicken or the egg? Are they razzing you because you're being rude or are you being rude because they're razzing you?"

"You sound like a guidance counselor."

"I'm being serious," I said. "I like the Pamela I'm talking to now. The one who is patient and funny. And I think a lot of the other kids would like her as well."

"All right. All right. Enough of this stuff," she groaned. "You sound like Mr. Rogers. Give me a break."

"It's true."

"I said 'enough.' We'll see you tomorrow."

Once again, I called Chris when I got home, to tell him of my progress. I let him know about my increasing skill and how Pamela had let me out of the skit. I wondered why I didn't feel more relieved than I did.

"That's great," Chris said. "But I think you'd better watch out for your mom."

"What do you mean?"

"She phoned me tonight and asked if I had a skateboard."

"She did? Why?"

"She asked me what kind of board I owned and if you'd been using it."

"Oh, no," I groaned. "She's got to be suspicious."

"I threw her off, though," Chris said. "I told her

the truth. I told her that you'd never used my board. I told her I'd never even seen you on a board. I wasn't lying. So if she *was* suspicious, she won't be now."

Mom didn't say anything to me that night, so I guessed that Chris was right. He must have thrown her off.

I guessed wrong.

Chapter Seventeen

Go to Your Room

Steve Powell came up to me at morning locker break. "A buddy of mine was walking through the park last night. He tells me you were practicing with somebody."

Did Steve know that Pamela was teaching me?

"So you do got a board after all?" he went on.

I wasn't going to tell him it was Pamela's board.

"My buddy only watched you for a few seconds. He says that you were doing some fakies. Are fakies enough to make you junior ramp champion in Montana?"

I still didn't say anything.

"I think you got nothing," Steve asserted. "I still think that you're going to look mighty anemic on Saturday. Then I'm going to enjoy myself with two hundred big ones. And, oh yeah, it's going to make me real happy to see my sister drop you."

"We'll just have to see what happens, won't we?" was all I said to him.

I was pleased to see that the initial hype over the contest had died down. Although some of the seventh grade kids were still wearing Marissa's tags, they weren't cheering every time they saw me.

Marissa was pleased when I told her that I wasn't going to do the skit with Pamela anymore.

"That's only right," she said to me at lunch. "People like us just don't do that. I don't know why you'd even think of working with her."

"Pamela isn't that bad," I defended.

"She must be a disappointment to her mother. I mean her mother is a doctor. It's too bad she can't cure Pamela," she told me. Then she started to laugh as if she'd just heard the funniest joke in the world.

When I told Mr. Eshenko, he was more than a little upset about the switch. But he cooled off when Chris and I explained it to him. It didn't mean that Pamela was going to have to do a monologue. I was. Chris was now going to be Pamela's partner. Chris wasn't too happy about that, but when he protested at my suggestion, I quickly pointed out that he owed me for trying to save his two hundred dollars.

Pamela was definitely more low key than usual. She smiled at me a couple of times, but didn't say anything.

The big surprise of the day was waiting for me at supper.

Mom had made a cheese casserole that had taken a long time to cook. I was anxious to get over to Pamela's place to practice and was gorfing through my dinner.

"I hope you're not going to eat like that tomorrow night," Mom complained. "Alison has invited a friend back for supper, a delightful little boy."

Alison mouthed the words "Rotten Roger" to me.

"Why are you eating so quickly anyway?" my mother wanted to know.

"I got to go out again," I told her. "I'm going to Pamela's place. To practice." I figured that my mother would think that I meant the comedy sketch.

"I see," she said. "And how is the skateboard practice coming?"

I stopped chewing in mid-bite. "De skadeboard pracdise?"

Mom put down her cutlery and folded her arms across her chest in menacing-teacher fashion. "Yes, the skateboard practice. I assume you're going to see Pamela because you're able to skateboard over there. Is she teaching you?"

"Iz see teadin me?"

"Swallow what's in your mouth, Jordy," Mom ordered. "And I don't want to hear any more lies. I'm not a stupid person, you know. The other day, Mrs. Boyer came to school wearing a tag that said, "Go Jordy, Go." She thought I'd get a charge out of it."

I swallowed. "Oh, no."

"Oh, yes," Mom went on. "It seems that there *is* a skateboard contest this Saturday. And it seems that Jordy Shepherd *is* going to be in it. In fact, he's become quite the seventh grade champion."

"Oh, no."

"Why did you lie to me, Jordy? Why have you been skateboarding?"

Alison looked down at her dinner, waiting for Mom to get really angry.

I sighed. "I don't know why I lied, Mom. I got myself caught in something and this seemed to be the only way out. I'm sorry. I've never lied like that before."

"Why didn't you come to me with your problem?" she demanded.

"Because you would have been upset with me. Like you are now. You would have been disappointed. Like now. And you wouldn't have let me skateboard."

"I see. And you've been going to Pamela to use her skateboard?"

"She's been teaching me some tricks," I confessed.

"Then I want you to go to your room," she said sternly.

"Go to my room? You've never sent me to my room for doing something you didn't like. Look, Mom, let me tell you the whole story. Let me tell you why all this happened. You see, it started last Friday at Steve Powell's party . . ."

"I'm not interested. Go to your room."

"Mom . . ."

"Now, Jordy."

I chucked the napkin on the plate and fought back the wetness that was building in my eyes. "You don't know what will happen if I don't enter the contest. I'll be nothing at my school. Worse than that. And Chris will . . ."

"Go to your room!" she snapped. "Now!"

I pushed away from the table and obeyed the order. I was finished. Everything had just fallen apart. There was no way I'd be able to face the kids at school again. No way at all. My only exit had closed.

I pushed open my door and wiped at the two tears that had managed to escape.

And then I saw it on my bed.

A skateboard.

And what a skateboard, a Howlin' Heavy Ramper. There was a yellow and green spider painted on the top deck. The trucks were chromed and the wheels were the same yellow-green. I picked it up and gently spun the wheels. The ball bearings spun silently.

"It's yours," my mother said from the doorway. "I tried to phone Chris last night and get some idea about skateboards, but he was so vague. The clerk at the store recommended that one. I hope you like it."

I looked at her and then at the board. "It's terrific, fantastic . . . but . . . I don't get this."

"I'm sorry I was so rough with you at the dinner table, but you deserved it for lying to me. I wasn't going to let you off the hook without some display of my displeasure.

"But why the board?"

"The other night, when I was lecturing you, I called you a young man."

"I know. You use that when you're really upset."

"Then when you got angry at me, I realized that you are, indeed, a young man now. And perhaps I've got to let go a little bit."

"I . . . I don't know what to say."

"When I discovered you had lied, I was extremely upset," my mother went on. "Then I wondered why. I wondered if the fact that I had dragged you halfway across the country had something to do with it. I know that you didn't want to come. And I didn't give you any opportunity to express your views. You were happy in Great Falls and I uprooted you."

"It's O.K., Mom."

She shook her head. "No, it isn't. I should have listened to my young man. So, I said to myself, 'Jordy must have a good reason for lying, for doing something against my wishes. If he is growing up, then this is an opportunity to show my trust.' That is why you have the skateboard. It's because whatever your reasons, I trust you."

"I can tell you how I got involved in this," I said.

"Not now, please. This may sound silly, but this is a big step for a mother. At least, for this mother. Tell me your reasons next week after the contest. If I heard them now, I might think they were silly and I don't know how I'd handle that. I might want to give motherly advice, rather than trusting your judgement.''

''Everything's going to be fine, Mom. Thanks.''

''You're welcome, Jordy. From now on, I promise to listen to you. And I want you to promise that you won't keep anything like this from me again.''

''I promise,'' I agreed. ''And then, we hugged each other and for some reason that made me cry as well.

Chapter Eighteen

Learning to Slam

"What an incredible board," Pamela said when she saw my mother's gift. "Do you have any idea how much a Howlin' Heavy Ramper costs?"

"Would you like to try it?" I asked.

"You'd let me use your board?"

"Why not? You're letting me use yours, aren't you?"

"Mine's old. Besides it was part of our deal. This is a new board. It's never been on a ramp before."

"Then it should be initiated by the best." I smiled.

We had to wait a half hour for some kids to finish on the ramp. Once they were gone, Pamela scrambled up the stairs and dropped in. For the next several minutes, she went through her moves . . . fakies, grabbing air, hand plants, and a few new ones that she described to me. Every time she cleared the lip, the yellow-green wheels glowed in the street lights. The hum and swoosh of her routine was almost musical . . . as if she was singing on the board. Talk about poetry.

When she finished her nose was covered with tiny beads of sweat. "Thanks," she said as she handed my board to me.

"You looked great."

She took a deep breath. "It's like I'm in another world when I'm doing that."

"It makes me wonder why you've never entered a skateboard contest. How come nobody knows how good you are?"

She shrugged. "I don't know. It's not important. Besides, it's guys like Steve Powell who are into it. You know, Joe Cool and Company. And it's balloon-heads like Marissa who jump up and down and giggle and cheer. Who needs that?" Then she paused. "Sorry what I said about Marissa."

"Not everyone who's into skateboards is Joe Cool and Company. Look at me."

She laughed.

"Do me a favor, Pamela. Think about entering on Saturday. It'll impress a lot of people."

"So what?"

"So, they'll look at Pamela Loseth in a different way."

"And then they'll like me?" she scoffed.

I shook my head. "They'll sure see another side of you, won't they?"

"I just don't do that stuff."

"Think about it, that's all. It would be important to me."

"You know, Jordy, you're the one who's different. You're nice."

"Most people are. If you give them the chance."

She shook her head. "I'm not sure how many people would have done what you did in English class. Thanks for setting me up with Chris in the comedy skit. It saved me from being a center-shot again."

"No problem. Can I ask you something personal?"

"I guess."

"Promise you won't get upset?"

"I can try."

"Why do you wear those glasses?"

She huffed up, then relaxed. "I don't know. They're weird. They suit me."

"I don't think so. I think you'd look better with a different style and color."

"I think you look better in your cowboy boots and jeans."

"Guess I deserved that one, didn't I? Sorry. If you like your glasses, that's all there is to it."

"Since we're being truthful, let me tell you that I've been thinking about what you said yesterday," she told me. "About the other kids razzing me and stuff. It won't work. I can't change. I can't be someone I'm not. I'm always going to laugh funny. I'm always going to say what I think."

"But maybe, some of the time, you could just *think* what you think."

"Maybe." She smiled. "Once in a while, maybe . . ."

"And you could let everybody see the side that I've seen."

"Maybe . . ."

"But don't try to change the laugh," I told her. "That's a gift. It makes you special."

"Thanks for saying all that stuff, Jordy."

"Hey, we're friends."

She sniffed and then laughed. "These kinds of conversations aren't helping you learn to wipe out. Let's get busy."

So she taught me how to drop in. It wasn't as hard as I thought it was. It was harder. The first three times I tried to nose my board over the lip I ended up skidding down on elbows and knees. In spite of the pads, I took a healthy bashing.

"It's in the head," Pamela instructed. "You're tensing up. You're thinking about falling. Go do some fakies and a couple of one-eighties. Think about what you do when the skateboard slows and is about to fall back in. That's what you do when you drop in.''

I built up my confidence inside the ramp, then I tried another drop in. Success. My bruises thanked her for the lesson.

After I'd semi-mastered the entry, Pamela told me how I was going to fake my injury.

"This is how the contest works," she explained. "Each skater has to do a forty-five second run. You fill out a routine card and hand it to the judges. There's three of them. This tells them what you're planning to do. The tricks have different degrees of difficulty. Grabbing air is tougher that a fakie and so on. The judges watch you and see how closely you follow your routine, then they rate how well you did. Each judge can give you a maximum of thirty points. They average the scores. Twenty-five is a good run.''

"If I wipe out, I get nothing?" I asked.

"No, you lose ten points a pop. That's why you have to hurt yourself before you finish your routine. Then it's just a "no go." Almost everyone starts with fakies and moves into one-eighties and their varia-tions. Only a few kids will do any serious air work. I don't think Steve will. And I'll be surprised if any-one in junior does a bodyjar. It's tough and too easy to slam. Your run will be fakie, one-eighty, body-jar.''

"Wait a minute," I said. "The bodyjar is where you land the trucks on the lip, right? You spread the wheels on the tubing. How can I fake that?''

"As I said, it's a tough trick. If you hurt yourself trying it, it'll look realistic. But, at the same time, you got the least chance of really hurting yourself.''

"But it's an air trick?''

"Sure, but you're landing on top. Not in the ramp. So you're going to land on the top platform. You're only going to fall two feet instead of eight."

"I don't know . . ."

"When the board goes airborne hold onto it and as it falls, stand up. Let it hit the grind and slam yourself on the platform. There you are, twisted ankle, unfinished run; you're out of the contest. It doesn't matter how well Steve does. He'll never know who won because you got hurt trying a tough stunt."

"I don't think I can make it realistic," I said. "I'm just not good enough to do air."

"You're not doing air, are you?" she reasoned. "You're pretending to do air. Besides it's like dropping in. If you relax, it's easy."

"Easy for you to say."

We had to stop for a while because a couple of elementary school kids came to use the ramp. But once we had the park to ourselves again, Pamela showed me how to sail past the lip, grab the board and land on the platform in a sprawl. "Just remember you're only two feet up. Don't think about the bottom of the ramp."

So I worked with one-eighties until I had enough courage not to turn at the top. I let the board sail into mid-air and dove at the platform on top of the ramp. I made a big production of hitting the plywood surface.

"Not bad," she coached. "But you forgot to grab the board. You can't do a bodyjar without a board."

"Where did it go?" I moaned.

"Judging by the speed, it's in orbit," she laughed.

Next time I remembered to grab the board, but forgot to bring my feet down.

"You're going to hurt your shoulder that way," Pamela advised.

"I already have," I groaned.

A half dozen attempts later, I was doing a fairly decent imitation of Pamela's controlled wipe out. I was bringing my board in line with the lip before falling off.

"It's good," she told me as I stood up from my last slam. "It's real good. See, I told you I'd teach you. Do it again."

I shook my head. "No, I'm getting too wrecked. Tomorrow."

"It may be tough to get time on the ramp tomorrow."

"We'll take the chance. I'm hurting."

"O.K.," she agreed. "Come back to my place and I'll show you some street tricks. I'll show you how to pick your nose."

"Huh?"

"It's a trick where you bounce the nose of the board off the curb. Nose-picking."

I started to laugh. "Nose-picking? Can you teach me to pick my nose?"

She ha-horked. "Nobody can teach nose-picking like I can. I'm one of the best nose-pickers on the planet."

Chapter Nineteen

Why Does Your Nose Hurt?

Friday morning went smoothly. A few kids wished me luck on Saturday, but most were more interested in the football game. Flower Valley High was playing its first home game in the afternoon and the junior high was closing so that we could watch.

In English, I worked on my monologue. It was funny, but I had enjoyed working on Why, What, and Bug Off more. I noticed that Pamela was trying to teach Chris the routine we'd made, but he was having a tough time understanding the whys and whats.

The football game was terrific, 45–10 for Flower Valley. Reese made his debut as quarterback, threw two TD passes and ran in for another two himself. I hurt my throat cheering for him.

Marissa held my hand during the game. And that felt terrific as well. Kind of. It was fun being with her, but we didn't seem to be saying all that much to each other.

I asked her if she'd like to go to a movie with me on Saturday night. "There's a funny movie called *Guppy Love* at the mall," I told her.

"That might be a good idea," she agreed. "Let's see how well you do in the contest first. I mean, what if Steve beats you really badly?"

I wondered what she was going to do when I slammed. For some reason, it didn't really bother me all that much anymore. I still wanted to go out with her, but it didn't seem as important as it had a week ago.

When I got home I heard this terrible screaming noise from the living room.

"Hello, Jordy," Mom called from the kitchen.

"What's that?" I asked. "Who's screaming?"

"That's Roger," she told me. "Alison asked him to dinner, remember?" Then she shouted, "Keep it down in there, kids."

The howling continued.

"Maybe you could ask Roger to be a little more quiet," Mom suggested.

I went into the family room. Alison was sitting on the couch while this freckled face kid with a huge nose and wide, blue jammers was charging around the coffee table and yelling at full volume.

"Hi, Jordy," Alison shouted above the noise. "This is Roger."

"Hello," I said.

"ARRRRGGGGHHHH!"

"You want to be a little more quiet, please," I asked him.

"ARRRRGGGGHHHH!"

"What's he doing?" I shouted at Alison.

"He's being an airplane," she shouted back.

"Why is he so noisy?"

"He's a jet."

"ARRRRGGGGHHHH!"

"This is tower control," I yelled at Roger. "You are cleared for a landing on runway two. Land now!" Then I grabbed him.

He stopped and continued to yell for several more seconds before he broke into a great smile. "I was going fast," he bragged.

"Glad you've landed." I let him go and shook his hand. "I'm Alison's brother."

He laughed. "You want to see me be a cow?"

I thought about that for a few moments. "No, that's O.K.," I told him. "But thanks anyway."

"How about a wounded water buffalo?" he asked.

"A what? A wounded water buffalo? Where do you get this stuff?" As much as I was interested in seeing that, I decided that this kid should be kept calm.

"Let's play Monopoly," I suggested.

That was a disaster. The rules of Monopoly are completely beyond the understanding of the six-year-old mind. I had to tell them what to do every move. And Roger kept taking money from the bank and stuffing it in his pockets. I was pleased when Mom called us for dinner.

I like Mom's fish and chip dinner. She makes her own batter and cuts her own potatoes and then deep fries everything. Then she cooks Green Giant canned peas until they go all soft. Alison calls them "mushy peas." Roger was obviously delighted with the menu choice because he took great quantities of everything.

"Would you like me to come to the skateboard contest tomorrow?" she asked me.

I'd thought about that. Part of me wanted to show her how I could fakie and one-eighty. And another part knew that when she saw my slam, she'd take a bird. All her suspicions about skateboards would be confirmed. "Would you like to come?"

"The truth is, I think I'd be too nervous. I'm not sure what you're doing, but I'm sure that it would look dangerous to me. I'd rather just wait for you to come home in one piece."

"Sure, Mom, I understand."

"Anyway," my mother said. "We mustn't ignore our guest. Tell us about your family, Roger."

I turned my attention to the little guy and knew right away that something was wrong. He was rubbing his eyes and making these disgusting sniffing noises. Alison was giggling.

Roger looked distressed. "It hurts."

"What's the matter, dear?" my mother asked.

He picked up his napkin and tried to blow his nose. Alison continued to giggle.

"Don't be disgusting," I said.

Roger started to whimper. "It hurts."

"What hurts, dear?" Mom asked.

He pointed at his nose.

"Your nose hurts?" Mom asked.

He nodded and then started to cry.

"His nose hurts?" I wondered out loud.

Alison began to laugh.

"Why does your nose hurt, dear?" Mom asked.

"He put peas up there," Alison told us.

"He put a pea in his nose?" Mom's voice was barely audible.

"Not a pea," Alison corrected. "A whole bunch of them. Roger is so funny."

We ended up taking him to the emergency room. Doctor Loseth was on duty when we arrived. She removed seven peas from Roger's nose with a pair of tweezers. When she asked him why he'd put them up there in the first place, he said, "To see if they'd fit."

His mother came to pick him up. She didn't seem surprised or upset. I guessed it was just another day in the life of Rotton Roger.

Later, Pamela and I only managed to have about fifteen minutes on the ramp before other kids came to practice. I slammed a few more times and felt that I was 'on top of my game.'

We ended up at her place watching TV, eating popcorn and laughing about Roger.

"Sounds like someone I'd really like," she told me.

"He's definitely different."

"Then I'm sure I'd like him." Pamela laughed as she pretended to shove a piece of popcorn up her nose.

"Why are you laughing?" _____ _____ repeated.

"We don't know." Pamela _____, "I guess you'll

Chapter Twenty

A Slam

Saturday was a perfect day for the skateboard competition. Warm, blue sky, wispy clouds. I wished it were raining.

I passed the morning watching cartoons with Alison. And as each McDonald's commercial ticked away another fifteen minutes, I lost more and more of my confidence. So what if I'd managed to learn to roll back and forth in a half-pipe ramp? So what if I'd managed to fake a couple of half-decent wipeouts? That was at night with just Pamela watching. There would be all kinds of people at the park, including Marissa and Steve Powell. Was it possible to convince that many people?

Roger's father phoned Mom at lunch. He said that the little guy's nose was much better. Then he told her that their family was going to the contest and Roger would like Alison to come along. Would that be all right?

"I think that would be nice," Mom agreed.

"Looks like you got a new friend," I said to Alison when I heard the news.

"I just hope he doesn't do nothing stupid," she said.

Mom told me that she was sticking to her plan to stay away. "Good luck, Jordy," she said as I was leaving. Then she added "Be careful," and repeated it five times as I walked out the door with my skate-board in hand.

I knew there was going to a crowd, but I wasn't prepared for the hundreds of people in the park. They were sitting in lawn chairs around the ramp or on blankets on the hills. It looked like the whole town to me. I figured that my mother was the only one who wasn't there.

I noticed a couple of paramedics leaning against the side of an ambulance. My first thought was that I hoped I wouldn't need their services. Then I realized that when I faked the slam, they were going to take care of me.

I sighed and watched an elementary kid doing a routine on the ramp. He seemed so relaxed, so sure of himself. Surely, when it was my turn, everybody would know I was useless. My brain was trying to convince my legs that they should run away, when Chris greeted me with a big smile.

"Hey, you're right on time," he said. "The young kids are almost finished. Everything is on schedule. The juniors are set to go at two."

"There's a big crowd," I noted.

"Like I told you, skateboarding is a big thing in Flower Valley." He slapped my shoulder. "So how you feeling? You all excited about this?"

"Excited? I'm scared."

"I was thinking," he said. "When you wipe out, you're still going to be a hero. Kind of. Marissa will think you're real brave for hurting yourself."

"I'll never pull this off," I muttered to myself.

"Hi, Jordy," Pamela joined us and handed me a plastic bag. "I brought my extra pads and helmet."

"Thanks. I'm glad to see you," I told her.

There was something different about her. It took

me a few seconds to realize that she was wearing different glasses. They were smaller with thin red frames.

"You like them?" Pamela asked.

"They look super. The red suits your hair."

"Thanks. My mom bought them for me this morning. I wore the others because they were so different, so strange. I'm still going to wear them, they're old friends, but only once in a while."

"And I'm going to wear my jeans and cowboy boots. Once in a while."

We grinned stupidly at each other.

"Am I missing something here?" Chris wanted to know.

Neither of us answered him.

"You scared?" Pamela asked me.

"Very," I confessed.

"Me too," she said.

"You too? You mean you're going to enter?"

She nodded. "Junior girls are at three-thirty. Will you stay to watch?"

"You bet I will."

"See you later?"

"See you later," I agreed.

She smiled and moved off into the crowd.

"What's all that about?" Chris wondered. "Are you and Pamela . . . ?" Then he laughed. "No, that's a stupid thought."

"Speaking of stupid thoughts," I said, "it was one of yours that made this happen. I want you to promise that you're never going to start with the bragging bit around me again."

"Sure, sure," he agreed. "Reese has been telling me that all week. I'm straight now."

"I'll believe it when I see it."

"Hey, poser!" Steve Powell came toward us.

"You know," I said. "I'm getting really tired of hearing that."

"We're going to find out in the next few minutes, aren't we?"

"Don't you have to go grease down or something?" Chris said.

"Huh?"

"Get lost," Chris explained.

Steve laughed. "In a few minutes, I want to see your two hundred."

The PA broke up our discussion. "Attention. All boys entering the junior contest are asked to register at the desk now. All boys, age twelve to fourteen, please register now."

We headed to the registration table near the playground. "What are you doing?" I asked Chris.

"I'm going to enter too. I'm not that good, but it's for fun, right?"

"Only for some of us," I disagreed.

I signed up and received my routine sheet. I filled in my moves—fakie, one-eighty, bodyjar . . . then I threw in some side and back air. What the heck? I wouldn't get that far anyway.

After the elementary kids finished, we were called over to the judges table and handed in our sheets. Then we picked our number from a goldfish bowl. My piece of paper read "14," which meant I was second last. I was hoping that I could get it over with quickly. Now I was going to have to wait longer.

"Hey, I'm number one." Chris held up his number for me to see. "The best go first, right?" he joked with the judges.

I noticed that Steve Powell had drawn number five.

"Competition begins in a few minutes," one of the judges told us.

The fifteen of us were ushered to a roped-off area reserved for the contestants. Steve Powell immediately started doing stretching exercises. That's because he has to go for the whole forty-five seconds, I thought.

I looked at the crowd as I slipped on the pads. I saw most of my homeroom. In fact, I saw most of the school. Mr. Eshenko waved at me when I noticed him sitting with his little kids. Alison, Roger, and his parents had a good spot just to the left of the ramp. They were too busy eating a bag of chips to see me wave at them. Marissa was sitting with Jennifer. She blew me a kiss and then she and Jennifer started laughing. To my disappointment, I couldn't see Pamela.

"Number one," the PA announced.

Chris slapped my hand and climbed the stairs to the the platform.

"Chris Williamson," the PA told everyone. I heard people cheer, the timer buzzer sound and Chris dropped in.

He did some fakies, a few one-eighty variations, but no air work. There was polite applause after he was finished. The judges awarded him 17 points.

"Not bad huh?" he said when he returned.

The next person added a rock 'n' roll on the grind. He got a 22. And that remained high score as the next two skaters did similar routines to Chris's.

"Number five," the PA barked.

Steve hurried up the stairs. When his name was announced there was a wild cheer from the crowd. Every ninth grade kid in the audience was on his feet and cheering. Steve held the skateboard over his head to display the graphics and turned around slowly to acknowledge everyone.

The cheering got louder.

"Look who's posing," Chris grumbled.

Steve placed his board on the lip, nodded at the judges. The timer buzzer howled and he dropped in.

Chris had told me that Steve wasn't that good, but he was sure better than the guys who'd gone ahead of him.

He didn't even bother with fakies, but went right into one-eighties. Then he did a rock 'n' roll and dropped back in.

"He's got much better," Chris told me.

Steve shot up the side and grabbed side air. The audience hooted and applauded.

"Much better," Chris repeated.

Steve did a trick that Pamela had told me was a method boneless, then he shot up the side to grab more air. The board cleared the lip by a good three feet. He grabbed the deck, tucked in his legs and got ready to drop in.

But he kicked out his feet a fraction of second too soon. The back wheels snagged on the grind and Steve dropped in a mass of arms and legs into ramp.

Everyone, including Chris and me, stood in a collective "Ooooh." Steve bounced down the side and rolled into the center of the U. His face was scrunched in pain and he moaned. A paramedic started to climb onto the ramp, but Steve waved him back.

Slowly, he staggered to his feet. He looked around as if he was dazed and grimaced when he put weight on his right leg. A ribbon of blood trickled from his nose and he wiped a red smear over his lips and chin.

Then he turned over his board, pushed off and finished the last ten seconds of his routine with three fakies. I'm sure that's not what his routine sheet listed. When the timer horn sounded, everyone—ninth graders, seventh graders, Chris, me—applauded.

Now the paramedic jumped onto the ramp and helped Steve down the side and over to the ambulance. We were still clapping when Steve sat on the back bumper, waved an O.K. sign to us, and let the attendant wipe his bloody face.

"How was that for an act of courage?" the PA called. People cranked their appreciation another few decibels.

"Maybe it would be a good idea if you could make yourself bleed as well," Chris suggested.

"The judges awarded Steve Powell 17 points," the PA declared. "That means that if he hadn't slammed, he would have received 27."

Another round of applause.

How was I going to make my fake wipe out look real now, I wondered? After Steve's courage, I would only look like a wimp. Even though I was so close to ending the mess, it sure wasn't getting any easier.

Chapter Twenty-one

Number Fourteen, Jordy Shepherd

Several skaters later, a limping Steve Powell returned to the competitor's area. Most of the guys congratulated him. He acknowledged them with a nod.

"You were good," I called.

He glanced at me for a moment. Then looked away and sat on the grass.

A short time ago, I was disappointed because I'd wanted to go first. Now I was glad that I was second to last. I wished that my turn would never come. I wondered if I could possibly fake an injury climbing the stairs.

"Number fourteen," the PA called. At first, it didn't register as my number. My turn couldn't have come so quickly. Chris elbowed me. "That's you, Jordy."

"What happened to number nine?" I asked.

"He's gone," Chris anawered.

"Number ten?"

"He's gone already."

"Number eleven?"

"It's your turn," my friend insisted.

"I think I'm going to have a heart attack," I mumbled.

"That's normal," Chris assured me. "Go for it."

Go for it, I thought. *Go and pretend to wipe out.*

"Number fourteen," the PA repeated.

I clipped on the chin strap and made my way to the ramp. As I started to climb the stairs, the cheering began. It started as a low roar and climbed through medium roar into a symphony of calls and whistles. By the time I reached the platform, every seventh grade student in the crowd was hollering. A group of people from my homeroom where holding up a banner that read, "Jumpin' Jordy—#1 Thrasher." Another group started to chant "Go, Jordy, Go."

"Jordy Shepherd," the PA announced.

The cheering rose higher. I saw Marissa clapping her hands and laughing with Jennifer. Mr. Eshenko tightened his fist and waved it at me. I still couldn't see Pamela.

I placed my board on the platform and the crowd noise stopped as if a volume knob had been turned to off. I looked at the mass of people, but no longer saw anybody. "All right," I said to myself, "let's wipe out and get on with your life."

The timing buzzer wailed and I pushed toward the lip and dropped in. The sudden acceleration sent a shot through my stomach and I sucked in a breath. I let the board drift to a stop and roll back down, back up, stop, roll down . . . my two fakies.

There were some shouts, but it was just noise. I concentrated on the board and the plywood. As I ascended once more, I leaned into a wide one-eighty, down, up, and into another wide one-eighty.

So far, everything was going well. I wasn't sure how I looked, but it felt smooth. "Thanks, Pamela," I thought. "Thanks for teaching me so well."

I picked up speed from the wide arc and sailed into a tight one-eighty. That further increased my speed and I quickly shot into another tight one-eighty. This was it. The board zipped down and shot up the other side of the half-pipe. Now, it was time to fake the slam.

I bent my knees and let the nose of my Howlin' Heavy Ramper go for air. The hum of plastic wheels on plywood became the muted whisper of rushing air.

My mind ticked off the points that Pamela had taught me: grab the deck, pull the board directly in line with the grind, lift from the crouch, let the board bounce of the grind, fall off.

I grabbed the deck with my left hand.

I pushed it underneath me.

I straightened my knees.

My board and I fell toward the grind.

I flinched for a moment. My mind knew I was going to thud into the platform. But instinct told me otherwise.

Suddenly, everything was clear and sharp, like the picture on a postcard. I was falling toward the grind. The grey plastic tubing was a distinct, definite line below the Howlin' Heavy. Directly below it. I was lined up perfectly. And instinct told my body to wait . . . to wait for the jar.

The board smashed into the grind and stopped. If I hadn't been ready for it, inertia would have sent me sprawling over the lip. But as the board bashed the plastic, I bent my knees as if I was jumping. I swayed left and right and then discovered myself balanced on my board with the wheels split on the tubing. A perfect bodyjar.

The cheering washed over me, a surf of clapping and yelling. For a few moments, I didn't move. Then, because I didn't have any idea what to do next, I stepped off the board, placed it back on the platform and dropped back in. I finished my routine with a few more one-eighties.

When the timing buzzer signalled the end of my run, I let the board slow into the center of the ramp. I picked it up and jumped down. The crowd was still cheering, although it was obvious from the number of people talking to each other that they'd expected something more spectacular than one-eighties after the bodyjar.

As I walked past the judges' table, one of the judges called to me. "What happened to the air tricks you have written on your card?"

"Next year," I told her.

"Holy jumping," Chris greeted me in the contestants' area. "I don't believe what I just saw. I don't believe it."

A couple of the other competitors congratulated me.

"And the points for Jordy Shepherd's run," the PA crackled. "A total of . . . twenty. That puts Jordy in sixth place."

"Twenty?" Chris said. "Twenty? Twenty! We won. You beat him. You beat Steve! We won. I won. I won two hundred dollars." Chris hugged me. "I won two hundred smackaroonies!"

"Congratulations," Steve was standing next to me. He held out his hand. "I'm not happy for you. In fact, I'm definitely pissed off. But it was a nice bodyjar. I guess you knew you had enough to beat me and didn't want to risk it with air tricks, huh?"

"It was just luck," I told him.

"Look, about that poser stuff. I thought I had you pegged. I get thick-headed sometimes."

"You owe me, Steve," Chris butted in. "You owe me two hundred."

118

"No, he doesn't," I said.

"You beat him," Chris reasoned. "You beat him. That means I get two hundred dollars."

"Think about it, Chris," I pointed out. "Think about our plan."

"But . . ."

"It was luck, Chris. We lucked out. You have no right to that money and you know it."

Chris kicked at the grass. "Well, I just . . . but . . . you're right."

"What's going on?" Steve wondered.

"Let's just forget everything, O.K.? The bet. The words. Let's just let it go."

"I don't owe you nothing?" Steve asked Chris.

Chris shook his head. "No, we're cool."

The last skater had finished and I discovered Marissa in the competitors' area holding onto my arm. "You won," she said. "It wasn't quite what I expected, but you did win, so I guess that means . . . you know . . ."

"That we're going out?"

"Yes."

"Not interested," I told her.

"What?" she exclaimed.

"What?" Steve and Chris echoed.

I pulled my arm free. "You and I don't have anything in common. You're only interested in me because I happened to get three more points than your brother in a contest I had no right to enter." Then I paused and looked in the crowd. "I can do better."

"Well, I . . ." she didn't know what to say.

I searched the crowd again, looking for Pamela. I saw her near the ambulance. She was standing with my mother.

"I have to go," I said.

I walked past the ramp and thanked the people who were shouting their congrats. "Hi, Mom," I said.

"My heart was in my mouth," she told me. "But I couldn't stay away. I'm proud of you, Jordy."

"Thanks, Mom." I smiled. "Wait until you see how good I do next year."

My mom turned to Pamela. "And I have to thank Pamela for holding my hand during your routine. I could barely watch. We were hiding behind the trees." Then she smiled and looked at both of us. "I think I should go and see how Alison is doing."

"She's a nice lady," Pamela told me after Mom left.

"I didn't know that you knew her."

"I didn't. I saw this lady peeking behind the trees and I said to myself, 'She looks a little like Jordy. I wonder if it's his mom?' So I went over and asked her. When she said she was, I figured I'd better stay close to explain about your fake wipe-out."

"Thanks for doing that."

"Turns out I didn't have to, did I?" she grinned. Then she punched my shoulder. "Hey, major thrasher."

"Pamela, would you . . . would you do the comedy skit with me on Monday."

"Me? Me and you? What about Marissa?"

"Bubblehead," I said.

She ha-horked.

"And would you like to go to a movie with me tonight?"

"Yeah, Dopey, I'd like that a lot."

"You ready for your run?" I asked.

"More than ready."

"You think I've got time to buy you an ice cream before you start?"

"Ice cream? There's always time for ice cream."

I took her hand and we headed toward the Dickee Dee cart. I saw Marissa standing with Jennifer. She had her fists resting on her hips and she was glaring at me. I ignored her.

Then I saw my mom and Roger's mother walking to the ice cream cooler as well. Alison and Roger were walking behind. Roger was picking his nose with both hands, a finger in each nostril. He seemed to be enjoying the process.

Looks like we've both found good nose-pickers, I thought.

MARTYN GODFREY is an ex-junior high teacher who wrote his first book on a dare by one of his students. Since that time, he has written over twenty books for young people. Many of the humorous incidents in his stories originate from his fan mail. "I get lots of letters from young people," he explains. "Most of them tell me of a funny experience. It's great reading about the silly things that happen to people." Besides writing, Martyn's hobbies include growing older and collecting comic books.